SHOOT TO KILL

SHOOT TO KILL

WADE MILLER

HarperPerennial
A Division of HarperCollinsPublishers

HarperCollins books may be purchased for educational, business, or sales promotional use. For information, please write: Special Markets Department, Harper-Collins Publishers, Inc., 10 East 53rd Street, New York, NY 10022.

First HarperPerennial edition published 1993.

Designed by George J. McKeon

Library of Congress Cataloging-in Publication Data

Miller, Wade.
    Shoot to kill/Wade Miller.—1st ed.
        p.   cm.
    ISBN 0-06-097483-4 (pbk.)
    I. Title.
PS3563.I421475S48   1993
813'.54—dc20   92-53390

93 94 95 96 97 ❖/RRD 10 9 8 7 6 5 4 3 2 1

To Jeanne

SHOOT TO KILL

CHAPTER 1

MONDAY, OCTOBER 1, 4:00 P.M.

He carried the evidence under his arm, thirty yellow pages bound into a green paper folder. On the cover of the folder was printed in darker green, SEABOARD INVESTIGATION SERVICE, but this was held against his coat so it wouldn't show.

Despite the October heat wave, despite his dislike for the job ahead, Max Thursday strode swiftly along Sixth Avenue and shoved through the glass doors of Weaver Sporting Goods. It was the downtown San Diego outlet of a local chain of four, scattered around the country.

It was prosperous enough to steal from. Thursday walked across thick carpeting and through moistly conditioned air, past racked rifles and rubber-booted dummies posing with fishing gear, and another dummy grotesquely naked in swim fins and trunks and diving goggles. Since it was a bad Monday, the first of the month, and nearly closing time, he had no trouble getting by the enervated clerks and entering the storeroom in back.

There Thursday sat down on a wooden crate of football helmets and waited. He knew Bliss Weaver, the boss, had seen him enter. He wiped the perspiration off his upper lip and loosened his undistinguished tie for the dozenth time that day and gazed idly at the gloomy stacks of spare goods and out-of-season displays, also waiting their turns.

Bliss Weaver entered suddenly. He was some five years older than Thursday, which put him past forty. He half-

1

grinned and said, "Too hot even to think business," and flexed his large powerful hands uncomfortably.

"Likely to get hotter." Thursday held up the green paper folder of evidence.

Weaver's handsome face tightened. "No doubt about it, huh? I always liked the kid."

"We made our final checkup Saturday. I guess you'd better call this Arnold Nory back here and I'll get it over with."

"I guess," muttered Weaver. He was a big man of football build with bushy brows and sandy hair that didn't show the gray. A man's man, and just as plainly a lady's man. Although wearing a thin open-necked Hawaiian shirt that hung loose around his trousers pockets, he managed to seem better dressed than Thursday in his sober business suit. Thursday's own bigness was mostly bony frame on which no suit ever looked quite reputable.

He had no reason to dislike Bliss Weaver but he did. Nothing personal, simply a type unlike his own. Weaver's private life had been in the papers too often, invariably concerning women. Perhaps Thursday's feeling was a natural male jealousy. Although Weaver was reputedly volatile and quick-tempered, he had proved easy enough to work for. He paid promptly, never haggled.

But now he hesitated, inspecting Thursday curiously. Weaver said, "I wouldn't have your job for a million dollars." Then he walked away with his easy animal grace.

Thursday shrugged and laid the green paper folder beside him on the packing crate and got out his wallet to hold ready in his hand. No, Weaver hadn't said, "A dirty way to make a buck," but he'd might as well have. Thursday sat waiting again, his tenseness making his gaunt features look crueler than usual, thinning his mouth, emphasizing like a predatory beak his strongly arched nose. He had coarse black hair which showed off the few gray ones at the temple—unlike Weaver's—and his eyes were blue, icy now—unlike Weaver's warm yellow-brown gaze.

2

Then Weaver returned to the storeroom with a third man. Weaver said, "Arnold, this is Mr. Thursday who wants to talk to you." He moved a few uneasy steps away, leaving the dirty job to Thursday, leaving Nory standing like a prisoner before a judge.

Thursday got to work . . . put him on the defensive . . . scare him, beat him down . . . humiliation . . . "I met you already, Nory. Saturday afternoon, when I bought a dozen softballs for my team."

Nory tried to look puzzled, saying how-do-you-do in a pleasant salesman's voice. He wasn't much past twenty, with a wise but deliberately open face of which his fun-loving red-lipped mouth was the most distinguishing feature. Brown curly hair was already receding to a sort of crest like a tiara above his high tanned forehead. "I don't remember the sale right off, Mr. Thursday. We had a big day Saturday and—"

"You remember," Thursday interrupted. "First, I feel duty-bound to tell you that I run the personnel checking service to which Mr. Weaver's stores subscribe. You or your clerks can't tell my operatives from ordinary customers. My people survey sales approach, cash handling methods—and honesty." In Thursday's hand his wallet opened like a pair of jaws. He turned the celluloid leaves slowly so Nory could read the impressive membership cards: World Association of Detectives; Associated American Detective Agencies; California Association of Investigators.

Thursday snapped the wallet shut, put it away. "So let's get to it. This downtown store has shown shortages this last quarter. You're the reason, Nory."

"Oh, no," Nory protested. "Now wait a minute, if you think you—"

"We not only think—we know." The young man's brown candid eyes commenced widening as Thursday picked up the folder of agency reports and leafed through the pages. Each yellow page was a printed form which had been filled out in longhand by one of four operatives or by Thursday himself in the case of the final survey Saturday. To the back of each page was stapled the cash register sales slip involved, if such had been properly given the pseudo-customer. Occasionally, between the pages was flattened the entire roll of detail tape from the register. If no sales slip had been given out, and if the detail tape (which recorded every sale rung up on the cash register during the day involved) didn't show the operative's transaction, then either a blunder or a theft had occurred. A blunder, of course, revealed itself in that day's cash balance; a theft did not.

Those particular yellow pages relating to Arnold Nory's discrepancies had their corners turned back for easy reference. "September 15," Thursday chose at random. "One of our operatives bought a paddleboard and a trident spear, total cost $138. The detail tape from the register shows that you underrang the amount at $118, a twenty-dollar difference which went into your pocket."

Already, Nory's young face was flushed and his breath came short. "That can't be so," he said incredulously. "Give me a chance to—"

"September 18. Our Operative 36 left a pair of badminton rackets for restringing. Charge is five dollars per racket. No service ticket was written out. You as assistant manager would be the one to check on such a discrepancy in the repair department, or to let it slip by."

Nory's lips trembled; no words came through. He dared an anguished glance toward Weaver, who looked away. Nory went back to staring fearfully at the hard-faced accuser who droned out the proof of his crimes.

"September 24. Our Operative 12 . . . " Thursday kept digging at the fool he had trapped, occasionally looking up from the damning pages to glare at him with cold scorn. Inside he was sick of himself. He could enjoy the work of trapping, but never this inevitable slaughter of another man's pride. Another yellow page, another glare at the scared victim, and Thursday decided Nory had been softened enough for the final arrangements.

". . . then last Saturday when I bought the softballs from

4

you. You laid the money on the cash register ledge without ringing it. Our Operative 24 cut in on my sale with the correct change for a baseball score pad. You rang 24's sale but not mine and pocketed the twelve bucks for the balls. Pretty dumb trick of yours but we'd made it easy for you." Thursday shook his head pityingly. "Any use going on with this?"

"No, don't," Nory moaned. "No, okay, I guess you know all about it anyway. I did it." In the background, Bliss Weaver sighed; the employer always found it hard to believe, probably because it was a blow at his own judgment. Nory looked around the store room helplessly. "What are you going to do to me?" he mumbled.

Thursday took a kindlier tone. "How long has it been going on? Let's see, you've worked here a year and a half—"

"No, not that long! I mean, I only started three months ago—about when I got my promotion. I just took a little I needed, and then it got so I needed more . . ."

"We figure you averaged about a hundred a week. Fourteen weeks, that's fourteen hundred dollars. Considerably more than petty larceny."

"What are you going to do to me?"

Thursday pretended to consider. "That depends on Mr. Weaver. And also on what you intend to do about it."

"I'll pay it back, pay it all back," Nory cried, seeing the straw held out to him. "You can trust me to—" He stopped, realizing the incongruity of what he'd said, then finished weakly, "I swear I'll pay it back, sir."

Another clerk came into the storeroom, saw the strained attitudes of the three men, and hurried out again. Thursday eyed Weaver, who murmured, "Naturally, if he wants to make it good . . ."

"I do," Nory pleaded. "I'll do anything."

Thursday had brought a piece of stationery with the Weaver Sporting Goods letterhead. He stood up and put the sheet on the packing crate along with his fountain pen. "Just write out a simple confession and a promise to repay. Put your name, address and the date on it."

Nory kneeled by the crate and began writing, after making a preliminary blob with the fountain pen and whispering nervously, "Pardon me." Thursday silently watched the young man, now actually on his knees, and thought how simple it always was and how shameful. It wasn't petty larceny but it was always a petty thief, frightened out of his wits. A criminal of any experience would have noticed that there had been no mention of police action, would have realized that the threatening attitudes were only a bluff, and would have walked out laughing at them. Taking this kind of theft to court was too difficult and too costly.

"Is this all right?" Nory asked humbly. He rose and handed the trembling paper to Thursday.

Weaver felt some of the shame of Nory's humiliation too. For he said roughly, "Why'd you do it?"

"I don't know. My girl friend needed the money badly—"

Thursday didn't listen to the rest of the excuse, which was the usual. They never stole the money to spend on themselves, to hear them tell it. But Nory's clothes were dashing and well-cut, considerably more expensive than Thursday's own. He glanced over what Nory had written.

October 1.

Mr. B. R. Weaver
While working for you in the last fourteen weeks I have made cash sales that I didn't ring on the register and kept the money for my own use.

I estemate the amount of money that I have stolen would be $100 per week making a total of $1400. If I am given a chance I promise to repay this money as soon as I am able.

Arnold E. Nory
3020 1st Ave., SD 3

Thursday noted the shaky handwriting, the nervous misspelling of "estimate." That too was part of the usual. He wrote "Witnessed:" at the bottom and signed his own name.

Then he turned on Nory again. "How much money can you pay back now?"

"I just got paid today. Here's the check." He fished it out of his pocket and proffered it to Thursday eagerly. "And I got about eight dollars in change that you can have." Thursday had him endorse the check, took it and an even eight dollars. He wrote the amount and date on the back of Nory's confession. He stacked everything, money and confession and the folder of agency reports, on the crate and told Weaver, "For your records."

Nory said, "This won't come out, will it? I mean, well, I was trying to get in the Air Force and you know—"

"Pay back the money and keep your nose clean from now on and you'll make out," Thursday said. "And if you'll take my advice, find yourself a girl friend with less expensive tastes."

Bliss Weaver grunted at this, and Thursday wondered if he'd put his foot in it. According to gossip, Weaver was currently having his own troubles with a spendthrift woman; a bitter fight over his divorce settlement was headed for the courts.

However, "That's good advice," was all that Weaver said.

Nory took a deep breath. He looked at the door and then at his former boss. As he sensed that the ordeal was over, the usual pattern broke down. The look Nory gave Weaver was nearly a sneer. Nory wasn't going to exit like a whipped dog. He squared his shoulders cockily, as if to tell them they could shove their advice, and said, "I take it you're through with me."

Thursday nodded, not feeling so sorry for the young man now. But Weaver stepped forward with a big hand outstretched. "Can't tell you how bad I feel, Arnold, that it happened to turn out this way. I never thought when I had you out to the house for dinner those times—"

Nory walked past the hand. "All right, I promised to pay back the money, didn't I? And if I could spit up those handout meals, this mere employee sure as heck would."

7

Weaver's tense restraint of the last fifteen minutes burst forth in temper. He grabbed Nory's neckie with one hand, drew back the other to hit him.

Thursday made a noise and lunged into it. He caught Weaver's fist, forced it up and back. Nory ducked out of it, and then Weaver tore away from Thursday. He didn't go after his ex-clerk again. He just stood there, eyeing Thursday furiously. And down his right cheek dribbled a little blood where Thursday's fingernails had accidentally scraped him during the brief flurry.

All three men were running sweat. Nory said, "Well, that's a fine thing," trying to look calm and amused.

Thursday said, "Get out of here. Don't come back," and Nory left. The storm in the air didn't leave with him. Thursday got out his handkerchief and mopped his face. "Sorry I had to stop that, Weaver. Especially since the smart punk deserves it. But you don't want to clutter up this business with an assault charge."

"No," said Weaver stiffly. "It's okay. You did the right thing."

"Sorry about that scratch."

Weaver was dabbing at his cheek with a forefinger. He looked at the smear of blood. "You did the right thing, let's forget it. I shouldn't have had the impulse to break his lousy neck."

He didn't sound forgiving. Thursday gave it up. "I guess we'd might as well wind this up. I've got a load of assorted sporting goods out in the car I'd like to return. I'll bill you for the service between now and the tenth, twenty-five dollars checkup fee per store and half of whatever's recovered from Nory."

"*If* anything's recovered from Nory. He hasn't learned any lesson."

"About two hundred and twenty-eight dollars have been recovered so far. We've still got his confession. I intend to work on him some more with that as soon as he gets a new job."

Weaver turned to a shelf by the storeroom telephone, took

8

down a pipe and began to pack it. There was a tremor in his big hands that didn't betray itself in his coolly polite voice. "I'm not saying you haven't done well, Thursday. I'm quite pleased with your results. I'll settle your bill promptly."

Thursday nodded and said goodbye. Weaver just nodded. As Thursday left, he was lighting his pipe, drawing at it viciously. Quite a temper after all, Thursday thought, and wondered if he was going to lose the account.

He walked through the store, sighed when he got out into the baking-hot late afternoon on Sixth Avenue. He felt dirty and unreasonably discouraged. He was glad the worst of the day was over. But it had only begun.

CHAPTER 2

MONDAY, OCTOBER 1, 5:00 P.M.

To give his girl friend time to get home from work, he put in a while at his own office, which was on the fourth floor of the Moulton Building, downtown. The frosted glass of the door told about him. Max Thursday—Private Investigations. Seaboard Investigation Service—Commercial & Industrial— Licensed & Bonded to the State of California.

The Seaboard business was a recent expansion and doing well. But it was not the ubiquitous far-flung network with which he had menaced Arnold Nory. Thursday could speak of an operative numbered 48, but only because Thursday numbered by 12's. And the four he hired were on a part-time basis only. Thursday kept up their state licenses ($120 per year per license) and they were on call when needed, principally because they couldn't resist their own cop blood. Two of them were former police matrons, now housewives. One was a retired prison guard. Another was an ex-motorcycle patrolman who had lost part of his hand in a traffic accident and who also doubled as a lifeguard during the summer months. Seaboard agency reports sometimes revealed an Operative 1, Thursday himself, who came in at the final stages of the larger investigations, as he had in the Weaver matter, simply to keep down the overhead.

Nor did he feel much like a big shot this evening, as he sagged around his lonely one-man office, listening to feet going home throughout the building, listening to the closing-hour traffic roar subside in the streets below. He jerked his tie even looser, fiddled with the trivia on his desk. Finally, after scrutinizing his bank balance, he wrote out checks for his operatives on the Weaver case and addressed and stamped the envelopes. When he commenced composing the bill for Weaver, he said aloud, "That's enough for one day," and got up and left it unfinished. Tomorrow would do; it always did. He felt morose and deeply rutted. Carrying his coat, he trudged downstairs, putting the four checks in the mail drop en route.

He was still darkly moody when, about six o'clock, he used his key to let himself into Merle's apartment. But he forced a grin for her sake, since the downtown hotel where she lived had been built before the days of air conditioning and he supposed she would be feeling the heat.

She was. She popped in, startled, from the bathroom and said, "Oh, for goodness sake! You scared me half to death!"

"It's just me. I couldn't scare anybody." Thursday ambled over and kissed her mouth casually. She kissed back the same way. Merle Osborn was a tall full-figured woman who could be nearly beautiful when she chose, which wasn't often. Tonight she was much as Thursday had gotten used to seeing her lately: brown hair pinned haphazardly on top of her head, a housecoat belted about her body, and her bare feet stuck into his bedroom slippers. Lack of makeup and undarkened blonde eyebrows did nothing for her almost perfectly round eyes, and her pale mouth was quirked in the same half-peeved way as his own.

After the apathetic embrace, she said, "I had a bath. Now I'm washing things. You didn't call or anything."

"Got busy and forgot." Which wasn't strictly true. She shrugged and went back into the bathroom. He parked his coat and called after her, "You eaten?"

"Not hungry. You go ahead if you want."

Thursday wandered into the close confines of the kitchenette and dourly inspected the contents of the refrigerator. He decided he wasn't hungry either, poured himself a glass of beer and returned to flop on the living room couch. He kicked off his shoes and tried for a time to make small talk with Merle but the water was running in the bathroom and neither of them could hear. So he gave it up and stared at the old familiar crack in the ceiling.

Merle emerged while he was lighting one of his new cigars. She gave it a sickened look but fetched him an ash tray automatically. "Sit down," he suggested moving his hips over.

She simply stood there, continuing with some obscure thoughts of her own. "It's getting so I could scream. And I remember the day when I used to break my neck getting to the office."

"The office" was a newspaper, the *Sentinel*, where Merle had held down the police beat for over five years. She was good at it; she had to be since crime news was the most important department on the strident *Sentinel*.

"Bored, honey?" asked Thursday whimsically. He trailed his hand up the backs of her bare legs under the housecoat. Since she'd just bathed, her round thighs felt pleasantly cool and powdery. He suddenly thought sentimentally how long he'd known Merle and the fun they'd had and what a shame they'd let it go unimportant lately. No wonder they both felt lost tonight.

"Don't!" she said quietly, and jerked away from him. He chuckled, thinking she was kidding. He pulled her down onto the couch with him and wrestled playfully, pulling aside the shapeless robe so that her long legs kicked nakedly. He kissed her, thumbed down the straps of her brassiere so he

11

could kiss her some more. Both brassiere and panties were dark blue lace.

"Oh, for crying out loud, Max!" whimpered Merle, and cuffed his ear stingingly and rolled free onto the floor. "Not in this weather!"

He rubbed his ear, decided not to be offended. She was right, it was too hot to enjoy anything. He watched her stand up and put herself together. "Where'd you get the lace pants, lady?"

"Quote me the ordinance that says I can't buy new underthings occasionally. Please quote it." She switched over and gazed sulkily out the window. "Furthermore, the shade was up."

"Oh. One of *those* nights," he said pointedly and picked up the evening edition of her newspaper and tried to interest himself in the sports page.

Less than fifteen minutes later, without turning away from the city lights beyond the window, Merle said, "I don't know why you bother to come here if all you're going to do is bury yourself in the paper."

He chuckled. "No, don't bother to apologize."

She flashed him a faint smile at that. "I guess business must be on the good side. At least, I certainly haven't seen much of you the last few weeks."

"Now, wait a minute. You've been the busy one, filling in on the desk for what's-his-handle. Don't blame me for that." When she hunched her shoulders impatiently, he added softly, "Come on over and relax, honey."

"You know how I love the smoke from old inner tubes."

"And you know why I switched to these things," he snapped back at her. His cigars were supposed to represent good business psychology, to make him look more like a Rotary member than the shady operator which most people thought a private cop must be.

"If you had to give up cigarettes, you might've tried pipe smoking. A pipe looks distinguished."

"Sure, sure." The last pipe he'd seen had been in the angry hands of Bliss Weaver. Which reminded him, "Say, speaking of business, I think I'm going to lose a client. That playboy you sicked on me a while back."

"Oh, Bliss Weaver. What about him?"

"I wound up a personnel check for him today and we had a little disagreement. He's got a temper like an itchy badger."

Merle turned around to eye him. "You're not one to talk, Max. You know, it's all in the way a person gets handled."

On that basis, he didn't dare start an argument. He merely grunted. "Okay. You knew him before I did. But you knew him on a different level, remember. You didn't have to please His Majesty. And it was also nine months ago when you were digging into that thing about his wife's stolen bracelet—"

"His ex-wife's."

"Wife then. And if the talk around the courthouse is right, she may be his wife for a long time yet."

"The talk *I* hear around the courthouse," Merle said sweetly, "is that he'll definitely get his divorce. And without giving her the shirt off his back, either."

"Since you hear all and know all, let's forget it. I've had a bellyful of Weaver today." He withdrew behind the newspaper again, wishing the world were different. He heard Merle flouncing around the apartment, no cheerier than he. She did some dishes in the kitchen and then she came and stood by the window some more and when she said, "Max," gently, he was surprised to find her sitting, all composed, in the chair that faced the couch.

"What is it, honey?"

"Max, I'd like to have a talk with you."

He agreeably dropped the newspaper, drained off his beer. "Shoot."

"I've been doing a lot of thinking. Maybe you have too. What I've been thinking is that we'd better call it off." When he didn't get it, she added anxiously, "You and me. Call *us* off."

He sat up astounded, and his stockinged feet kicked over his empty glass.

"Hasn't it actually gone on long enough now, too long?" she asked calmly. "Certainly, we'll always be friends but—"

"Merle, wait a minute! This is crazy. Just because it's hot weather and we're having bad moods, don't start saying a lot of things you don't mean, honey."

"It's not the heat. It's not merely a mood. I'm just tired of this whole situation and I think you probably are too, maybe not realizing it. And I'm not getting any younger—and this situation of not being married and yet not being single—"

"But we always figured on getting married eventually and—"

"When?" She shook her head slowly. She dug out a ball of paper handkerchief from her pocket and rubbed her nose. "No, don't tell me there hasn't been time for you to ask me. Max, it's been *over four years!*"

"Yes, it has," he said lamely. Helpless for an answer, he gazed blankly at her bare knees which had come uncovered. Reddening, Merle quickly pressed her thighs together and tugged the housecoat into place, clear down to her ankles. He growled, "Oh, don't get coy at this late date."

"Please, Max, don't be like that. I'm not mad or hurt or—in fact, I'm not anything any more, that's the sad part. We've run our course, darling. If you really loved me permanently you'd have seen that we'd gotten married a long time ago. And don't say it isn't too late now." She smiled faintly.

"Well, maybe I didn't figure I had to ask you in so many words. Maybe I figured that we understood each other after all this time."

"Only maybes. Don't fish, Max, please. I hoped you'd understand now."

"I do, you bet I do," he grated, and got to his feet. He loomed over her but he felt smaller than usual and his stomach churned. "I understand you've got yourself somebody else."

She looked up at him curiously. "Why do you say that?"

14

"I may be dumb as a detective but I'm not a moron. I've never seen anybody reach a decision like yours on pure theory, not without some other prospect in mind. New lace underwear, huh? There's another tipoff, sweetheart, in case you didn't know."

"Max," she said through pale lips, "I'd like this to be a friendly discussion. Don't make it dirty. Don't make it ridiculous by acting like a betrayed husband, especially considering—"

"Ridiculous, that's a good one! I'm not dumb forever. Why don't you give me the right answer instead of this runaround?"

"Oh, grow up!" she snapped, ready to cry, and they glared at each other across the small hot room.

The quiet knock on the hall door reverberated with the shock of an alarm bell. Merle's mouth dropped open and she scrambled to her feet, gasping plaintively, "Oh, no . . ."

But Thursday had already jerked the door open, to face the other man across the threshold. And he thought furiously how dense he really was. The other man was a pipe-smoker, of course, and an acquaintance of Merle's. He was the man Merle had stuck up for, the man she had insisted would get a divorce soon—Bliss Weaver.

CHAPTER 3

MONDAY, OCTOBER 1, 8:00 P.M.

Both men grunted hello automatically, mere polite and meaningless noises to cover the crude exposure of the moment. Uncertainly, Thursday stepped back, and uncertainly, Weaver came in.

"Bliss," Merle's strangled voice said, "not tonight, you didn't tell me—please, in a minute . . . " And she disappeared swiftly into the bathroom, closing the door behind her.

The two men, left alone, continued to eye each other like strange dogs. Weaver's sandy hair was crisply neat from brushing. His big frame was debonair in a gray tropical suit. He made Thursday feel short in stockinged feet, shabby in his wilted shirt. Weaver said, "I wasn't expecting to run into you so soon again, Thursday." The scratches on his cheek were only two thin lines of dried blood now.

"No, I'll bet you weren't."

"But I suppose now's as good a time as any. I suppose Merle's told you."

"It turns out that she fell down on the big news, after all. I got the first flash but no follow-up."

"Then I'll tell it," said Weaver quietly. "We're in love with each other. We're going to be married."

Thursday laughed.

Weaver's hands became fists. He balanced forward and spoke without moving his lips very much. "I don't like you to laugh. Not at us."

As if warned, Merle came out of the bathroom and by her appearing kept the two men apart. She had run a comb through her hair and darkened her eyebrows and shaped her mouth with lipstick. Thursday remembered bitterly that she hadn't bothered to do any of it for him. She said, "Bliss, please," and Weaver relaxed sheepishly. "And, Max, sit down so we can talk this darn thing over sensibly."

"No, thanks," said Thursday flatly. "I tried to talk sense a while back and all I got was double talk. I can't see why you had to lie to me, Merle."

"But it wasn't a lie. Everything I said was true. We haven't anything important for one another. And I thought it'd be easier for you to take if—"

Weaver cut in. "Darling, why do you feel you have to explain to him? He's got no claim on you."

"I want to, Bliss." She took hold of his arm and faced Thursday. "Max—Bliss and I are going to be married." Her eyes were bright and proud and her knowing face looked girl-ish, and Thursday thought she looked prettier than he had noticed lately.

"I already told him," said Weaver grimly. "He thought it was funny."

"Why not?" asked Thursday. He could feel the red fever-heat under the skin of his face, and the cruel grin drawing the skin tight. He felt a deep reckless desire to hurt somebody. "I've heard worse jokes. Except this one happens to be on Merle and that sort of spoils it. Who you kidding, Weaver? You're not divorced, not by a long shot. And even if you were in a position to talk marriage—your reputation is public prop-erty. So what's your pitch to Merle? I'd like to hear it."

"Max," she begged, "don't talk like that. I'm sorry I han-dled this thing so messily and hurt your feelings. But don't say things you'll regret later. Please don't strike back at me—"

"And who's he to talk about public reputations?" flared Weaver. "I happen to know he's been divorced, too. And whatever I may be, I think it's better than a professional spy and a professional bully!"

This time it was Thursday whose hands clenched shut for a fight. But he saw Merle's eyes, scared and begging. So he snorted and let it pass. He said to her, "If he really means to make you his third wife—which I doubt—you might remem-ber what he did to his present one. Slugged her in front of everybody in the Marine Room."

"Slapped her," Weaver corrected savagely. "What's more she deserved it, she was taking off her . . . Look, Thursday, not that I care what you think but just for the sake of the record: both marriages were my own mistakes and I admit it. The first was one of those college deals, way too young, trying to do the right thing and whatnot. The second time was two years ago on a buying trip to Akron. Joyce Shafto, she was a convention receptionist, good-looking redhead who liked a good time same as I. Trouble is, that's all she likes, that and what she cutely refers to as 'go-money.' We broke up six months ago

17

after that Marine Room fracas. I agreed to give her—"

"Spare me the details," said Thursday. "I'd hate to break down crying for you."

Weaver gritted his temper between his teeth. His voice flattened out. "I gave her five hundred dollars a month maintenance, more than plenty. Three months ago, when Merle and I—well, I asked Joyce for a divorce."

"Three months." Thursday looked at Merle. She flushed. "Thanks, dear."

"I'm sorry, Max. I despised the situation but we *couldn't* let anybody know." She let go of Weaver's arm, dropped her hands hopelessly. "Joyce has been making such a stink anyway, trying to take everything Bliss owns, and if it'd come out about me . . ."

"I don't mind a sizable divorce settlement, well worth it," growled Weaver. "But this is a blasted community property state and she wants half of the works, a half interest in the stores. I built that chain of outlets with my bare hands, Thursday, and no scatterbrained gold digger—"

"Very tender," said Thursday. "I can see why your women rush out and buy new lace pants at the thought of you. But do you mind if I don't like being used as a cover-up for your two-bit love affairs?"

Bliss Weaver swung fast. His knuckles smashed against Thursday's mouth, sending him sprawling, while Thursday's own reflex blow only grazed Weaver's cheek.

Thursday rolled to his feet in a red haze, ready to charge. But Merle was already in the middle, shoving wildly at Weaver, holding out her hands against Thursday's return. "Bliss! Max! Oh, stop it, stop it!"

Both men's glowering fury fell flat with the realization of childishness. Merle was crying. Thursday shrugged, avoided eyes, feeling foolish. His lip stung as if cut and, glancing down, he saw blood on the front of his shirt. And he had opened a new small wound on Weaver's cheek, above the earlier scratches.

Weaver was sharing his feeling of shame and foolishness. He muttered, "Sorry I did that—didn't mean to lose my temper." He pulled out his handkerchief to dab at the oozing scratch.

Thursday said nothing. He sat down and began to put on his shoes.

Merle stood sobbing into her wad of tissue. "Why can't we just be sensible, be nice to each other? Why do you make me feel cheap, both of you?" She didn't know which man to turn to, whom to solace. "Max, your shirt . . ." But she stayed nearer Weaver.

"It'll wash out. With cold water." Thursday couldn't think of anything else to be said. Weaver tossed him the handkerchief he was using and Thursday wiped the blood away from his mouth.

Weaver said carefully, "Merle's right. No point in fighting. We both love her and owe her that much, certainly. And if it'll make you feel any better, Thursday, I wanted her to break with you a long time ago—but she was afraid of hurting you."

Thursday didn't answer. He didn't want to look at either of them. For Merle was now standing against Weaver, face hidden against his lapel, his big hands patting her shoulders. Her long familiar woman's body pressed close against a stranger for comfort. Somehow he found his coat and at the door he said, "Goodnight," and that was all. He went down the stairs by habit, without really seeing them.

Weaver had been the quickest to anger, equally quick to get over it. Thursday's anger, harder to arouse, was not so easily dismissed. He felt its lava welling up inside him with every descending step. He hadn't slammed the door of Merle's apartment but he slammed the door of his car. He didn't drive away from his parking place across the street from the hotel. He sat there, clenching and unclenching his fists, staring up grimly at the yellow light of her window. Her shade was down now.

He'd been made a fool of. By both of them, and not just tonight but for months past. Merle had even recommended Weaver as a client, let him work for Weaver, be his employee and his patsy. And all the time the doublecross, the sneaking around behind Thursday's back, the cheap affair that was making a sucker of Merle too. His teeth ached, they were pressed so hard together. On top of everything else he had been knocked down tonight without even striking a good blow in return. Well, he could do something about that, at least. He'd wait for Weaver and they could settle this double-cross on even terms. Thursday glanced at his wristwatch; a few minutes past nine.

When he looked at his watch for about the fiftieth time, it was getting toward eleven. He was still waiting alone in the muggy night, and the anger still bubbled inside him. Thursday swore aloud viciously and his lip cracked open again. He licked its warm saltiness, then pressed the handkerchief against the cut. Which led to the discovery that he had two handkerchiefs, his own and Bliss Weaver's; he had neglected to give it back.

His attention distracted, Thursday missed his chance. When he looked up, Weaver was climbing into his convertible a half block away. There was nothing to do but forget about revenge—or to follow by car. Thursday had waited too long to forget.

Weaver lived farther downtown in the U. S. Grant Hotel, but he turned his convertible north toward the beaches. Thursday followed, making no attempt at concealment. Weaver didn't appear to notice; he took the speedway around the dark curving shore of Mission Bay to the ocean, through lights and signs of Pacific Beach and La Jolla, finally down the winding road toward La Jolla Shores. Screened by palms and pepper trees, the expensive home area of rambling ranch dwellings and glassy moderns was only slightly cooled tonight by a feeble salt breeze. A quiet neighborhood of many walls and few streetlamps. The Beach & Tennis Club (in whose Marine Room Weaver had struck his wife) dominated the south end of the Shores; the haughty apartment development called Marcliff ruled the north.

Weaver headed for Marcliff on its ocean bluffs. The development had been built on a wheel pattern, sleek two-story beach apartments radiating like spokes from a circular park which served as a hub. Garages clustered in a smaller flatter wheel, as if spawned. A labyrinth of smooth private roads veined their devious ways among buildings and lawns and fan palms and children's play areas.

Not knowing Weaver's destination, Thursday lost him in the labyrinth, spotted him again—once again too late for the brutal accounting his pride demanded. Weaver's broad back was just disappearing into a building entrance.

Thursday parked his own car and sat considering the doorway. The surf beat softly on the beach below, lulling the anger that had drawn him through the calm night. He began to get curious, and then hopeful. Why was Weaver visiting out here this late at night? Thursday's cruel smile began to dawn again. Was it possible that Weaver was running true to form—could he be playing around with another woman besides Merle?

He slid out of his car and sauntered up the stone steps, on Weaver's trail. He found himself in a small round foyer, newly painted ochre, an apartment's redwood door on either hand, more stone steps leading up to the apartments above. Lights showed under the doors, and somewhere near orchestra music played. Thursday checked the mailbox names. When he read the name for Apartment 4—above, apparently—he tasted disappointment. The name slot held a calling card for Joyce Shafto. Weaver was calling on his estranged wife.

As Thursday scowled there, he heard a door overhead bang open and then heavy footsteps on the stairs, descending. But they were uneven footsteps, unlike Weaver's confident stride. Thursday dodged to the rear of the foyer where a back door opened into the night, unwilling to encounter a stranger.

But it was Bliss Weaver who came unsteadily down the stone stairway. Thursday saw him in profile under the foyer lamp. His face looked drained of blood. He passed through the front entrance and was gone, and Thursday made no move to follow. Curiosity had won its battle with anger now. The fight could wait. He wanted to find out just how Joyce Shafto had managed to shock her husband so.

Midway up the stairs, his nostrils twitched at a new smell that was neither salt breeze nor fresh paint. Escaped gas, only a wisp, then vanished. Thursday forgot it almost as soon as his mind classified it.

For the door to Apartment 4 stood wide open, the lights were burning brightly, and even before he reached the top step he could see into the middle of the living room where the redheaded woman lay in a dead heap.

CHAPTER 4

MONDAY, OCTOBER 1, 11:45 P.M.

She had been strangled. Thursday bent to touch the flesh of her arm. Still warm, from departed life or from the weather. He stood over the pitiful defenseless body, hearing his own live heart beat in his ears. He found he was rubbing his throat where there was nausea. He had seen the violently dead before but he had never hardened to the sight.

Joyce Shafto wasn't a pretty woman any more. Over on the television console stood a bare-shouldered laughing portrait of what she had been, a piquant thirtyish redhead whose face showed more good fun than good sense. The photo emphasized what had probably been one of her proud points, a long slim creamy throat. Now the long neck was totally bruise-dappled from jaw to collarbone. In a face blotched with broken blood vessels, her once-gay mouth stayed open in a mock grin, her tongue sticking through hideously. A terrible parody of the portrait, scarcely recognizable.

Thursday shuddered, remembering the latent power in Bliss Weaver's big capable hands.

Then, responding to his training, he drifted silently through the apartment, looking at everything, touching nothing. Everywhere the furniture was gray combed plywood, low and rectangular, innocent of ornament. The woman had known that she was the ornament. The woven rush squares of the carpeting whispered under Thursday's feet as he prowled. The light was on also in the bedroom but nothing seemed out of place. He saw his grim intruder's face pass by in the long frameless wall mirror over the vanity table. On the other side of the central hall he found the dark bathroom with its pagan corner tub. The dinette and kitchen branched off the living room. Another living room door led out to a night-shrouded sun deck but it was bolted from the inside. There was no rear door.

Which meant that the strangler, coming and going, had used the same door Thursday had entered, and which still stood open. A shiny night-chain latch hung beside it. It had probably been unfastened to admit death.

He saw the rumpled *Evening Tribune* on the wide Holly-wood sofa, the low gray cabinet next to it where two drawers had been pulled out as if a search had been commenced and then abandoned. All so calm and peaceful—but for the contorted face of the red-haired woman staring up from where she lay on the coarse matting.

Thursday squatted, studied Joyce Shafto bleakly, trying to be insensate. She wore no stockings, nothing under her tight gown. (He had seen her hose and underclothes tossed carelessly on the bed in the adjoining room.) She was attired neither for an ordinary visitor nor for an evening alone. She wore a gleaming party dress, a green evening gown with a single strap over her left shoulder. The daring dip of the gown over her pointed breasts indicated that the strap had been vital. No wedding ring or any other jewelry.

Her flesh was cooling now. Touching her that second time, Thursday noticed the scratch inside her forearm, a short red mark within the elbow bend. Possibly caused by a fingernail, just as his own nails had marked Weaver's cheek.

Thursday could reconstruct the tragedy wholesale. After a long tense discussion with Merle, Bliss Weaver had sped to La Jolla to have a showdown with his estranged wife. Perhaps he had phoned ahead from Merle's place; that might explain Joyce's seductive attire, part of her argument. It would explain, too, why a lone woman would unlatch her door at such a late hour.

A few minutes with Joyce—perhaps she had laughed at his showdown—and Weaver's overtaxed temper had broken out in murder.

Yes, it was a perfect fit, the predictable end of Weaver's uncontrolled passions, and Thursday felt a surge of personal anger. Not at the strangler but at the man. Here was his climax, this man whom Merle wanted to marry, whom she loved and trusted. The blow which was about to fall would crush her completely. No matter how she had lacerated his pride and feelings earlier tonight, Thursday could derive nothing but pain from the thought.

Beyond Joyce Shafto's body he could see the telephone crouched on its corner stand. It was five steps away. Five steps, dial the familiar number, ask for homicide. This is Max Thursday, I'm at Marcliff, a woman's been murdered, yes, I know who did it, how do I know . . . ?

Thursday stood up straight while the logic of questions and answers marched relentlessly through his mind, leading inevitably to the sordid revelation of Merle's liaison with the murderer. ("You know," they'd say, "another of Weaver's women. Say, that guy could . . . ") Thursday's hands were

24

sweating. Did it have to be inevitable? Bad enough for Merle that her beloved had turned out to be a murderer—did her battered emotions have to be made public property too?

Thursday mopped his hands with his blood-smudged handkerchief. As he held the wad of linen in his palms, the idea began to sprout inside him. Merle *could* be protected to some degree. All that was needed was for Thursday not to volunteer as a witness. Yet he was the only witness, as far as he knew, and Weaver had a price to pay. Thursday didn't intend to shield a murderer.

He turned his back on the beckoning telephone, pulled from his hip pocket the other blood-smudged handkerchief— Bliss Weaver's handkerchief—and knelt beside the dead woman. He worked the cloth between her curled fingers, pressed her hand around it, and stood up with a scared glance at the open apartment door. He hadn't been seen. The planted handkerchief would carry a laundry mark, enough evidence to tie Weaver in his crime, enough insurance that he wouldn't escape the price. These sudden planless crimes were always the hardest to crack and Thursday didn't intend that killer's luck should work for Bliss Weaver.

He left with hurried caution. He got down the stairs, out of Marcliff without being seen, and took frequent deep breaths driving home. He was clear of the Shafto murder now, and so was Merle. Perhaps Weaver would try to drag her in as an alibi, but that sort of performance wouldn't set well with her friends at headquarters. No, Merle was out of it—publicly, anyway. He'd never tell her what he'd done tonight. She'd get over Weaver pretty soon.

When Thursday had climbed into his bed at his duplex flat, he didn't expect to sleep. But he did in a fashion, a gray void shot through with vague frights. He got up at two in the morning, his naked body dripping sweat. He smoked a cigar, gulped down a nembutal. Nothing helped. He dressed again and walked around his block in the still morning air, a few lights winking at him from the harbor. He cussed out his own foolishness. Why had he meddled in a murder? Weaver had written out his own fate. Who was this wise guy Thursday, who came along adding touches?

When he came to his garage door, he knew where he was going. He backed out his Oldsmobile and sped back across the slumbering city to La Jolla Shores, to Marcliff. But there he stopped short of his destination.

All the windows of Apartment 4 were lighted now. As he watched upwards, the living room windows pulsed brighter with flashbulb explosions. A black-and-white prowl car stood in front of the building and beside it a black detective car. A white ambulance purred up and ghostly medics carried a stretcher up the steps.

Thursday's mouth set grimly and he turned homeward again, trying not to think of anything but what he'd done for Merle's sake. Yet another thought lingered deep in shadow, insidious in its hidden triumph.

"I sure took care of Bliss Weaver."

CHAPTER 5

TUESDAY, OCTOBER 2, 8:00 A.M.

When the doorbell jolted him awake the bright morning sun was already streaming in through the venetian blinds. Thursday wrapped a bathrobe around his long body and staggered barefooted to the front door.

In the blinding outdoor glare on the slab porch, Merle Osborn stood looking through the screen at him. Her normally piercing eyes seemed almost as bleary as his own. She wore one of her tailored workday dresses, the usual button missing. She mumbled, "I had to come—I didn't think you'd still . . . "

She came in when he unhooked the screen for her. He scooped up the morning *Union* off the porch but its headlines abridged politics, not death; the paper had gone to bed earlier than he. Thursday cleared his morning throat, groggily reminding himself he wasn't supposed to know about Joyce Shafto. "Sit down. I'll start the coffee."

When he returned from lighting the percolator, Merle still stood, alien and unhappy, in his middle-class living room. She said illogically, "No, I can't stay. I have to do *something*. I need your help."

That blew the fuzz of sleep away. "Sit down," he ordered. He didn't like what was coming. He hadn't expected her to come to him like this.

She sank slowly into a straight chair she'd always hated. In a sudden burst, "Max, the police have Bliss! They've arrested him! They think he killed his wife!"

Watch it, don't give yourself away, Thursday warned himself. "Did he?"

"No, no. Everybody thinks so except me. I know he didn't."

Thursday didn't comment or encourage.

"I've been up since five," she went on, oblivious to his silence but looking to his expressionless face for strength. "They got me out of bed to go cover the story. I didn't even know what it was till I got to headquarters. After that, I stuck around because I wanted to see Bliss. But I didn't, not really, no statement allowed—he just grinned at me, passing by, and he shook his head meaning that I wasn't supposed to know him. Then they took him into the jail and . . . " Her strained voice trailed off in a shudder. "I went back to the office and quit. Max, I couldn't write about *him!*"

"Somebody's going to." That was at least noncommittal.

Not quite crying, not quite rational, Merle continued to recite what she knew, and Thursday could think of no non-committal way to stop her. And the details, particularly those he knew firsthand, had a morbid fascination for him. The body had been discovered by a downstairs neighbor. The neighbor—who had apparently seen a good deal, Thursday speculated uneasily—had sighted Weaver leaving Marcliff last night. And the police had acted quickly.

"Not so good," Thursday said automatically when Merle stopped talking. His brain was chewing over an irksome thought: he hadn't needed to plant Weaver's incriminating handkerchief after all.

"Oh, he's such a fool," Merle said dully. "Not telling them the truth. He's made up some crazy story—just to protect me."

Thursday grunted, having other ideas as to Weaver's motives.

"The marks on his face, the ones he got when you two had that fight at the apartment. Bliss claims that Joyce made them, that they quarreled and she scratched his face and then he left. Can't you see how the police must go for that one?"

"Maybe Weaver figures the truth wouldn't sound any better, his fighting over another woman."

"That's not it, not what *he's* thinking. He's thinking he's got to protect my good name. My good and cheap dirty name." Merle shook with a sudden dry sob. "And I can't do anything to help him."

"Too late to help him now. You should have stopped him last night. You knew the mood he was in."

"I didn't let him—I didn't know he was going." Which didn't fit Thursday's preconception, but it was only a trifle. Merle was staring at him, her mouth open. "Why, you really think he did it, don't you?"

"Does it matter?"

"Yes, it does, oh yes, Max." Her eyes widened with anxiety; her voice stumbled. "The reason I came here—I know I haven't a bit of right, not after the way we broke up, but you did use to say you loved me . . . will you get him out of this, *prove* he didn't do it?" Once started, her plea came in a flood.

"I know you can do it. I know how much you can do, I've seen you before when things looked hopeless and, oh Max, Max, I need you so much, please say you'll help me, help him—"

"No," said Thursday flatly.

Merle stared at him.

"No," he repeated loudly, his face reddening. "I'm surprised you had the guts to ask me. I don't owe Weaver anything. Even if I did, I'd think twice about mixing into a murder case. On top of that, it's my professional guess that Weaver did kill her. It's against my principles and beyond my ability to clear a guilty man."

"But he didn't kill her! I couldn't be so wrong about him. I know we've hurt you with what we've done, he and I, but don't kick us when we're down."

"I'm not kicking anybody," he defended himself angrily. "So Weaver's an innocent man—fine. We've got an excellent police department whose job it is to tell innocent men from guilty ones. Okay. It's not my job."

Merle came storming to her feet as the telephone jangled. He turned abruptly and went into the kitchen to answer it. As he said, "Thursday speaking," he could hear Merle in the other room, "First time I ever heard you turn down anybody who needed help badly—well, I know why you're doing it, too—generous big-principled Max, always claiming to be such a sucker for a sob story . . . " He heard her burst out crying.

In his ear the telephone spoke in well-modulated cheerful tones. "Mr. Thursday, this is Ivah Hecht." The man spelled it out. "Bliss Weaver's attorney. I take it you've heard of our client's trouble, haven't you? I discover that you've been retained by Bliss in the past and I'd like to get together for a talk with you."

"I'm sorry, Mr. Hecht, but there's no use wasting our time. My work for Mr. Weaver was in another connection." Thursday became aware of Merle stifling her sobs to listen. "Murder's no assignment for a private detective. The police are perfectly fair and capable."

"In this case, man, there are certain aspects the police—"

"No. Very sorry." The coffee began boiling over on the stove.

"Well, perhaps you can recommend someone," said Hecht uncertainly.

"None of my colleagues would appreciate it. It's not the sort of job that men without official status like to tackle." They said goodbye, hung up, and Thursday rescued the angry coffee. He poured a cup for Merle. She stood near the front door, her eyes wild and bitter. "Here, make you feel better."

She slapped the cup out of his hand and called him a coward.

He sighed and stepped back out of the pool of hot coffee and began picking up the pieces of cup. "I don't quite see any reason for that."

"You and your lying reasons." She laughed scornfully. "You don't want to help, you want Bliss to be guilty. You want him out of the way. Maybe you think with him gone you can have me again, just like that. You won't. *You never will.*"

"Don't overrate yourself," he snapped.

"Oh, I won't. I'm nobody, just a cheap piece who tried to beg for the first time in her life. I don't think so much of me." She looked down at him picking up fragments of chinaware. "I guess you're the one I overrated." She left quietly, not slamming either door or screen, and it was more hateful than if she had.

He drank a cup of coffee for himself and it trembled in his hand. He knew Merle was overwrought and dead wrong. He'd never seen her so upset. She ought to understand he couldn't go into a murder case, work against the police. (Yet he was already in it, he'd been to the crime and had planted the killer's handkerchief there . . . yet if no one knew but himself . . .)

He was cleaning coffee stains off his carpet when the telephone bell startled him again. The voice saying, "Max?" was a friend's voice but it gave Thursday an unaccustomed chill. The friend was Lieutenant Austin Clapp, chief of homicide.

"Tried your office and got your telephone service," Clapp said genially. "That's a fat life you lead."

"Overslept. You do it on the city payroll too."

"You heard about the Weaver thing, Bliss Weaver? They got me up at midnight with it. Matter of fact, that's why I'm calling you." Thursday felt the chill again. "You been working for him, haven't you?"

"Just personnel checking. Nothing to do with his wife."

"Oh, I figured that. But there's some inside angles I wouldn't mind talking over with you, since you did know him face to face."

As if Bliss Weaver's fate were a whirlpool and Thursday could fight its currents for a time but not forever. He sighed and let himself be sucked in. "Okay," he said. "Where'll I meet you?"

CHAPTER 6

TUESDAY, OCTOBER 2, 10:30 A.M.

Marcliff in the morning had a postcard look, the young palms barely moving their fans to the sea breeze, the lawns sparkling in an unbelievable green beneath tall lazy rotating sprinklers and the insistent sun.

Thursday parked next to the black police sedan. Above, Austin Clapp leaned over the wall of Joyce Shafto's sun deck and called, "Come on up. Number 4, on the left." Thursday climbed the stone steps reluctantly but he was somewhat cheered by the broad grin on Clapp's face as they met in the apartment doorway. The detective-lieutenant was Thursday's height but ten years heavier. Patches of steel gray were edging out the brown in his hair, and his blunt face showed the official lines of his profession but his eyes were sharp and lively, despite a full night's work. Clapp was feeling good; he had his man. He wore his panama jauntily and carried his coat thumb-hooked over one shoulder.

Joyce Shafto was gone, of course, and Thursday couldn't hear any police work going on. "You all alone?"

"Crane's down below, getting some of the neighbors on record. Rest of the boys went home to bed. Sit down, Max, see how the other half lives."

"Dies" is the word, thought Thursday. He was full of morbid notions. He settled gingerly onto a gray plastic chair and looked around, as if for the first time. Yesterday's *Tribune* on the sofa hadn't been disturbed. The cabinet drawers hadn't been closed and Joyce's photograph still laughed at the world from atop the television console. The police lived by police time of a single violent moment, and they were very solicitous of that moment.

"First society murder we've had in some time," commented Clapp, wandering about. "Look at everything so spick and span. Not like the usual side of the tracks."

"Times you're a bigger snob than the D. A.," said Thursday. "Why'd you drag me out here? Can't you crack it by yourself?" He mustered up a grin and made as if to get one of his business cards from his wallet.

Clapp snorted. "This one cracked itself. I got nothing to brag about. But I do have a curiosity or two left. About Weaver, you worked for him, how'd you describe him, Max?"

"Well, he acts like . . . " Thursday hesitated, then was surprised at his own lack of assurance. "Uh, I don't know him well, just through business. I'd say a rather uneven type, I guess, used to getting his own way. Might raise a fuss if he didn't. Big enough to get his own way mostly, though."

"Uh-huh. I suppose you got the poop on last night from

Osborn." Clapp had his back turned and missed seeing his start of surprise. "But there's still some the press doesn't have yet."

Thursday relaxed. Of course, Clapp didn't know of Merle's relationship with Weaver; he was merely assuming that Merle the police reporter had tipped Thursday with trade gossip as she had plenty of times before. He grunted.

"Well, he choked her all right." Clapp pivoted away from the window view, blinking sun from his eyes. "For that matter, she'd been asking for it. Not that you see me sticking up for *any* murder or murderer, understand—there's always a better way out—but sometimes I wish our laws were set up a little more equitably. Divorce laws, I mean. She was pretty much a tramp, as I get it, and she liked to dig her spurs into Weaver just to see him buck."

"Maybe he wasn't such a prize to live with either."

"Doc Stein says he grabbed her so hard that the small bones of her larynx are crushed. You got to be pretty mad and pretty strong to do that. Ever notice Weaver's hands? Big and rugged." He asked suddenly, "Something happen to you?"

Thursday found that he was unconsciously exploring with his tongue the cut on his lip, still slightly swollen from Weaver's punch. "Nothing. Cold sore, bad one."

"Anyway, Joyce Shafto was home all evening, apparently alone. This is according to the people directly below—Apartment 2, name of Folk; Mrs. Folk found the body—who heard the television going earlier and heard her moving around off and on."

"When was the body found, by the way?"

"About midnight." Clapp grinned. "What you're thinking is right. The Folks are a pair of plain old-fashioned nosy neighbors, don't miss a thing. Mrs. Folk just happened to look out her front blinds and see Weaver get in his convertible, leaving. She'd seen him and his car before on other visits and she knew the whole story about how Joyce wouldn't give him a divorce. So presently she just happened to trot upstairs to borrow a television fuse—and see what she could pump out of Joyce. Weaver had left this door open. Otherwise, Lord knows when we'd have found her because the people in Number 3 opposite are in Guadalajara on vacation."

"Hurray for neighbors," said Thursday. He had barely missed meeting Mrs. Folk himself.

"They have their uses at times. Joyce hadn't been dead too long when we got here, not over an hour or two. Stein says the time of death fits fine. And Joyce had obviously been expecting her husband, though Weaver denies they had an appointment, says it was a last minute idea on his part."

"Why 'obviously'?"

"Follow this, Max. Joyce took care of her reputation here at Marcliff. The Folks say that Weaver was the only man who'd ever visited her here, day or night, as far as they know—and I'll bet they do know. See the night-chain rigged on the door? You know women alone. They don't open up for strangers."

"Maybe for another woman," suggested Thursday objectively. He was getting out of himself, simply a professional talking shop.

"Can't poke holes that way," Clapp said. "You should have seen the spread of finger marks on her throat. She wasn't strangled by any female unless it was a female ape. And look how she was dressed, an evening gown over nothing. That wasn't to receive a woman friend. Far as we can find, Joyce never made friends with women. Not the type. There's an older sister in Akron, Polly Shafto, that she was fairly close to. We've notified the sister as next of kin."

"Joyce didn't live in a vacuum."

"Certainly not, but she was discreet. Her bookie, whoever she used, didn't come to Marcliff. Her casual men friends, if any, didn't come to Marcliff. Incidentally, there's the husbandly angle to that evening gown. It's a green one-strap affair, one of those peekaboo types. Seems that she wore it to the Marine Room a few months ago with Weaver, the night they broke up, and kept letting the strap slip just to annoy him. He finally socked her and—"

"Slapped her," Thursday corrected automatically and surprised himself.

"Anyway, he hit her. So I figure, Joyce being the kind she was, that she put on that particular dress just to get Weaver's goat."

"Does Weaver admit that, getting his goat?"

"Mostly. Maybe you'd like to read it for yourself." Clapp searched inside his coat for a folded sheaf of legal size tissues which he passed to Thursday. "Transcript of his talk with the D. A."

"Already?"

"Early this morning. Got Benedict out of bed again." Clapp chuckled as he reslung his coat over his shoulder. "But Weaver insisted on making a statement. Very calm, very cool. You know, Max, when Crane and Bryan went to his hotel to pick him up he was sitting in an easy chair with Joyce's picture—the same pose that's here—on the floor in front of him. He was drinking whisky out of a thing from his pewter collection and smoking his pipe. Wasn't surprised at all, merely denied strangling his wife and came along quietly, depressive-like. He was already dressed, probably hadn't undressed. Go ahead, read it."

The transcript was at least a fourth carbon. Thursday skimmed through the formal preliminaries, the identification of District Attorney Leslie Benedict as Question, and Mr. Bliss Weaver as Answer. He hastened to the meat of the interview.

Q: What time did you reach your wife's apartment?

A: I don't know exactly. It must have been after eleven. I didn't look at my watch.

Q: Weren't you taking a chance, not having an appointment?

A: I didn't think about that. Joyce—she never went to bed before two. I wanted to talk to her, that's all.

Q: After she admitted you, how long did you talk? Did she object to admitting you, by the way?

A: No, she didn't try to keep me out or anything. I didn't

pay any attention to how long we talked. Maybe five minutes.

Q: Five minutes?

A: Maybe longer. Maybe ten minutes. I don't know.

MR. HECHT: If I may interrupt a moment. Bliss, you do realize that you don't have to spell out details, make this statement at all—

A: Sure, I realize that. But I want to.

Thursday looked up at Clapp. "Weaver did have his attorney there, then?" "Yes, Ivah Hecht. Seemed out of his depth. Oh, he's a good man, lots of high class trade, but not much criminal experience. I felt sorry for him, the way his client was spilling the beans. Benedict'll tear him to pieces in court."

Thursday nodded and went on reading.

A: We argued about the divorce. Then she got angry suddenly and hit me. These marks on my face. So I left.

Q: And Joyce Shafto—your wife—was alive when you left?

A: Yes.

Q: You didn't strike her in return? Or attempt to retaliate in any fashion?

A: No. I just left and went home.

Q: Regarding the scratch inside your wife's left forearm, opposite the elbow. Did you cause that while physically repelling her attack?

A: (no answer)

Q: Well then, do you remember touching her at any time, Mr. Weaver?

A: No. I don't believe I did.

Q: But she touched you, scratching you, seizing your coat pocket handkerchief during the struggle.

MR. HECHT: Pardon me. My client has denied the occurrence of a struggle.

Q: Encounter. Pardon me.

A: I don't remember her grabbing my handkerchief. Apparently she did. I didn't miss it. No, I don't believe I touched her.

That appeared to be all about the handkerchief and Thursday slowly let out his stored-up breath. And in the rustle of the legal flimsies he could almost hear the district attorney purring contentedly.

Q: However, your wife has been murdered by some one who did lay hands on her person. Who do you think did this, Mr. Weaver?

A: I don't know who her current playmates are. I haven't been interested. I haven't been interested since I got my first taste of her true nature. Several months back.

Q: I see. To sum up: you visited your wife unexpectedly, in a very short time you were quarreling with her, she struck you and you left without any retaliatory action. Although you admit striking her in the past. Immediately upon your departure, some other person entered the apartment and strangled her to death. Is that your construction, Mr. Weaver?

A: More or less. As far as my own actions go. But I didn't kill her.

Thursday skipped through the rest of the transcript. He thought he understood why Clapp had called on him for a candid opinion of Weaver. Because the prisoner's actions didn't make sense. He had insisted on a statement to the district attorney that would only help lock him in the gas chamber. He had freely admitted more than Benedict needed to convict him of Joyce's murder. Why then did Bliss Weaver bother to deny the murder itself?

Clapp was watching him closely. "Something bother you, Max?"

"No. Seems open-and-shut." He got up suddenly and wandered down the long living room to the cabinet by the Hollywood sofa. With the transcript he tapped the two drawers which stood open-and-not-shut. "Anybody ask Weaver about this?"

"It's in there, you must have skipped it. He denies opening drawers or touching anything. We didn't pick up any of his prints, for that matter. But he's lying. He must have looked for something and found it too. Joyce kept house pretty neatly. She wouldn't have left two drawers sticking out."

"Anything missing?"

"No sign of it. Truth is that Joyce didn't have any valuables left. We inventoried her pawn tickets, accounted for her wedding ring and various trinkets she used to own at the time she separated."

"In trouble financially?"

"Sure." Clapp went out to the kitchen wastebasket and came back with a copy of the *Union*, yesterday morning's edition. "She played the ponies hard. You know how many people get rich at that. Didn't find any old betting slips around, though."

Thursday traded the transcript for the newspaper which was folded to the handicap charts. They were confusingly annotated in pencil. "She must've had quite a system." He glanced toward the *Evening Tribune* on the sofa.

"Wasn't marked," said Clapp. "That's unusual because the *Trib* has more complete racing coverage. Makes me think that Joyce was excited last night, off her routine, maybe over a showdown with her husband. Which means that Weaver did have an appointment with her, no matter what he says."

"Or maybe she had company for dinner and didn't get a chance."

"She ate alone, according to the kitchen. There's a can of tamales opened and part of a glass of milk left. Autopsy'll confirm that." Clapp shook his head. "No, Max, except for the minor human discrepancies, it fits tight. Frankly now, can you go for that story? Can you believe that Weaver left his wife alive and that right afterward another man slipped in here and killed her? Remembering that the Folks saw *only* Weaver?"

"No." Yet Thursday felt his stomach contract. No, he couldn't believe it—but, in a way it *had* happened. He had entered the apartment after Weaver and hadn't been seen. Of course, he hadn't killed Joyce, she'd been dead when he arrived. *Hadn't she?* Thursday snapped his fingers impatiently, chasing the bad dream out of his head. He'd had nothing to do with the murder. "If it fits so tight, what's worrying you, Clapp?"

The opening door cut off Clapp's answer. Jim Crane came in, slapping his small loose-leaf notebook against his thigh. He was a detective-sergeant, Clapp's right hand, older than his boss, with white hair and mild blue eyes. The mildness was only a surface phenomenon; underneath, Crane was all cop. He blinked at Thursday, said, "Hello, Max, what's with you?" and to Clapp, "Austin, I'm ready to go."

Thursday murmured greetings and a weather observation. Clapp asked, "Didn't pick up anything new, did you, Jim?"

Crane grinned. "I can tell you everything that ever happened on the Folks' farm back in Iowa. As to the crime, not much. They were out on the beach all afternoon, came in about dinnertime. Heard Joyce Shafto up here from then on. They heard the doorbell ring up here last night about eleven. Undoubtedly this doorbell since it's the only one they can hear besides their own, same side of the building. Undoubtedly Weaver, they say. Once more around and Mrs. Folk'll swear she saw him do the job herself."

"How about the old babe in the other main floor apartment?"

Crane flipped pages in his notebook. "Miss Nancy Quinlan, spinster. Age is your guess, she won't tell you. Lives alone, thank you. Nervous type, keeps a light burning all night, and now it turns out that she had very strange portentous dreams last night." Crane closed his book. "A waste of time as a witness."

"Okay, Jim, I guess that does it. Take the car back into town. That's presuming Max will give me a ride."

Thursday said, "Sure." Crane nodded and left. Clapp said, "Any time you're ready, Max."

Thursday hesitated. "How much of a struggle was there?"

"Not too much, I figure. She scratched his face, got her own arm scratched back and then he choked her. Why?" Thursday pointed to the gray fragments of a small ceramic vase on the floor beside the telephone table. Clapp looked amused. "You're a detective—what do you make of it?"

"I'm asking you. And see over there." By the door was a dollar-sized smudge, resembling a dark lubricant grease, on the woven rush carpet.

"Maybe some of the boys tracked it in this morning. Maybe Joyce stepped in an oil puddle the last day or so. Who can tell? Remember not everything is evidence—especially that vase which I knocked over when I was phoning. Let's go." Clapp locked the apartment door behind them.

Crane had already disappeared in the police sedan. As Thursday drove out of Marcliff's groomed grounds, he said, "You never did answer me. Something's biting you."

"Nothing much. I've got my man." But he was brooding silently. They passed the Beach & Tennis Club, climbed the slope into La Jolla's outskirts. "Turn off here a minute, Max."

Thursday did, reached a white-fenced dead end on sheer reddish cliffs. Below, beyond the frothing surf, the inshore ocean was brassy green and beyond that, blinding blue until it became part of the sky. Clapp gazed at a freighter's smoke-curl beyond the horizon. "Wanted to ask you something."

Thursday thought, here it comes, Merle, I'll do my best for you. He braced himself. "Shoot."

"How close are you to Bliss Weaver? You good friends? For example, did he ever borrow anything from you?"

"No," said Thursday, not understanding. "I hardly knew him."

Clapp swung his head to stare at him. "Then why was Joyce Shafto holding your pocket handkerchief in her hand?"

CHAPTER 7

In that instant the car lurched toward the cliff edge and Thursday pushed his foot onto the brake pedal before he realized that the car hadn't moved at all. It was he who had given the convulsive start forward and he still couldn't get his breath.

"Gave me a shock too," said Clapp. "The dead woman had this male handkerchief in her hand and I supposed it was Weaver's. Ran it through the laundry-mark books and your name turned up this morning. That's why I called you."

Thursday found his damp hands were wrestling together as he tried to turn a cloudy muddle into thoughts. But the homicide chief's voice was not accusing him of anything; the voice wasn't suspicious. Thursday knew that all he had to say was that there must have been some mixup, that he couldn't explain it, and Clapp would shrug it away.

All he had to do was lie.

He made himself meet Clapp's inquiring gaze. Thursday said, "I'm glad it's out in the open. I had a lousy night's sleep."

"What's out in the open?"

"Let me tell you. Maybe afterward you'll oblige me by kicking my tail from here all the way into town. I pulled a crummy trick last night. On top of that, I butched it up." He dragged the other handkerchief out of his hip pocket and dropped it across Clapp's lap. "Here's the handkerchief she should have been holding."

Clapp's eyes were narrow now. "Don't stop there, son."

"That handkerchief in Joyce's hand—I planted it there. I was scared Weaver might get away with murder. You see, I followed Weaver last night out to Marcliff." To confess part was to confess all and Thursday listened to a flat shamed voice, his own, telling the whole messy story. About Merle, about his hating Weaver, about everything.

41

Afterward came a silence, Clapp's. Finally his mouth twisted bitterly. "Of all the dirty dumb stupid fool tricks . . . "

"Yeah. I know."

"*Do* you know? Do you realize you didn't trust me to catch Weaver without your lousy plant?"

"I didn't think that."

"What did you think of, then? Of how slick you'd get away with it? Poor Osborn! She's the one I feel sorry for, caught between two stinkers like you and Weaver. She's the poor kid who deserves better."

"I thought at the time I was helping her. I don't know."

"Don't lie to me or to yourself either. You wanted to get Weaver out of your way. You tried to frame him for murder."

"He's guilty." The rest was so mixed up, such a burden of nightmare, that Thursday couldn't deny it. In daylight, he couldn't be sure *why* he'd done it.

"Sure, he's guilty. That doesn't matter to a newly appointed God like you, though. *You tried to frame him.* Look at me! You're a law enforcement officer, huh? If any plain citizen did it, I'd have him up and have him hard. If one of my own men did it, I'd break him so fast he'd never know what hit him. What if you'd screwed things up so that Weaver had gotten away? Or flummoxed it so we couldn't convict him?"

Thursday had seen Clapp's anger before, but from the outside. He'd never had to writhe under it, without defense. He knew he was flushing shamefully, angry because there was nothing better he deserved. "Well, I'm not asking for any favors out of friendship."

"Aren't you? Listen, I'm in the spot, not you. That's what you've done. I got to take care of you out of loyalty, this one time I've got to. Doing that, I have to let my own principles go hang."

"No, let's go see Benedict," Thursday said wearily. "I'll lay it on the line." State license, state bond, and all. He knew dimly he was offering to put himself out of business.

"That'd do a lot of good," Clapp said sarcastically. "Right

now, Benedict's got a closed case. You poke in with your story and that'll be all that Ivah Hecht needs to confuse the issue, make a jury think maybe Weaver didn't kill her. A smart lawyer could prove you did it yourself just out of jealousy."

Thursday sighed. "Okay, what do you want me to do?"

"Not a thing. Stay out of it. Just think of your friends after this before you go off half-cocked."

"The handkerchief. It's bound to come up."

"I'll try to see that it doesn't. I'll steer Benedict away from it and I don't think Hecht has the criminal know-how to fasten on it. Besides, I wouldn't be surprised that Weaver's going to crack and try to cop a plea." Clapp scowled over it, considering. With Weaver's handkerchief he wiped the sweat off his heavy face. "If necessary, I'll take a statement that you trailed him to Marcliff, saw him enter and leave. That should wrap it up. We'll leave Merle out, won't challenge Weaver's phony story about the scratches."

Thursday wanted to say something more, about friends like Clapp being hard to find. He started to, but all that came out was, "Thanks, Clapp. And I'm sorry."

"Sure. Now." Clapp grunted. The long working night had begun to tell on him suddenly. "Maybe I'm doing it for the case, not you. Well, I'll take care of you since I've been trapped into being your accomplice. You tried to frame a man, for the love of Mike! You'll never be able to make up for that."

Thursday drove them back to town then and not another word was spoken but goodbye. From headquarters Thursday went on to a Market Street drive-in and had a cheeseburger and a malt. He scarcely tasted them although he hadn't eaten since early the day before. All he could taste were his thoughts. What if his handkerchief plant had worked and then Bliss Weaver had turned out to be *not* guilty?

"You'll never be able to make up for that," Clapp had said. The idea stuck with Thursday as he munched like a blank-faced machine.

Other cars came, lunched and left. The curvy tight-slacked

carhops trotted around the lot, providing and taking away, and overhead a twenty-four-hour neon sign flashed the letters K-D and Kar Dine in alternate red and yellow.

What if the handkerchief plant had worked? What if it had condemned an innocent Bliss Weaver? Thursday shook off the nagging possibilities but they buzzed back in swarms until he was being stung by the largest monster of them all: *what if Bliss Weaver was innocent?*

That was easy to deny. Bliss Weaver was plainly guilty. Clapp, a better cop than himself, was satisfied he had the right man. But that comfortable thought had a harsh echo—

Are *you* satisfied?

At last, grumbling to himself as if nothing more were at stake than a household inconvenience. Thursday climbed out of his car. He muttered, "Well, won't hurt to look into it. Won't change anything."

He slid into a phone booth as hot as a personal hell and as stuffy as the state gas chamber. He called the office of Ivah Hecht, the murderer's attorney.

CHAPTER 8

TUESDAY, OCTOBER 2, 1:30 P.M.

Only a rifle shot away on teeming Harbor Drive, the tan masonry of police headquarters thrust up its Spanish bell-tower. Thursday couldn't help giving its playful ruddy-tiled eminence a concerned glance as he walked out the pier to the Rowing Club. The Club—seemingly a congress of disparate white-frame buildings melted into one structure by the blazing sun—sprawled at the end of the pier on an island of mossy pilings. Green-shingled above, green thick-looking water below, the carefree edifice sported several levels of roof, a glassy backside, and some ponderous floats.

Thursday pushed through polished nautical doors and inquired at the desk. Ivah Hecht was in, as his secretary had suggested. An attendant led Thursday through the lounge and down a corridor to a large girdered exercise hall. Various game-court outlines were painted on the hard-wood floor and weight-lift grips dangled from the walls.

Only two men were present, both in club trunks, both slaving vigorously at the oar-handles of the two rowing machines side by side. Thursday had never seen Weaver's attorney. He advanced tentatively, footsteps echoing. "I'm looking for Mr. Hecht."

"Reprieved," sighed the smaller man gratefully and let go of the oar-handles. He was a Bacchus grown old, a rotund body pink with sunburn, a jolly red face with a circlet of white curly hair wreathed round his glistening bald dome. "I'm Ivah Hecht. I'm sorry, if it's about the launch, I've decided not to sell."

"I'm Max Thursday. Since your call this morning, I've been thinking. I'd—"

"Man, that's wonderful!" Hecht's smile had brightened to genuine pleasure. "There's plenty we can talk about, Mr. Thursday." His eyes flicked briefly toward his companion on the other rowing machine, then back to Thursday. "A pity I didn't know you were coming."

Thursday took the hint. "I'm in no big rush." A fib, when he wanted to blurt out, "Is Weaver guilty or not? Do *you* know?"

The other man had quit rowing to appraise Thursday keenly. "Thursday, huh? I've seen your ad in the phone book," he announced loudly.

"That so?"

"Sure thing. I know all about you private operators. I've got connections down at headquarters too. You've probably heard. I'm Kelly Dow." He put up a large sweaty hand to shake, which Thursday did. Kelly Dow was tall, brawny, and didn't appear nearly as elderly as Hecht though he must have been approaching the same age. His grip squeezed with hearty power.

"Don't get around much myself," Thursday said.

Dow shook back his mane of graying hair and laughed deeply as if at a good joke. He seemed to specialize in hair. His eyebrows were wildly bushy and his square jaw black stubbled and his torso thickly matted. His few patches of bare skin showed a heavy tan. Thursday sized him up as self-consciously virile, religiously virile, religiously keeping fit, and the club bore. "I'll bet dollars to doughnuts," said Dow, "that you're here on the Weaver case."

"I never gamble."

"Aha, what'd I tell you? Go ahead, Thursday, feel free to talk—I'm one of Ivah's suckers too. It's all in the family."

Thursday felt apprehension radiating from Hecht, who smiled through it all and said tepidly, "A pity we couldn't have arranged lunch together, Mr. Thursday." The attorney was plainly as anxious to discuss Weaver as Thursday was. But not in front of Dow, the outsider. Yet Hecht didn't dare to brush off Dow, the client.

So Thursday made some thin conversation about having lunched at a drive-in, and immediately, "Which one?" demanded Dow. Thursday, annoyed, told him and Dow gave his deep laugh. "Good for you! That's one of my places. Good old K-D Number One. K-D for Kelly Dow."

"That's clever."

"Course, I'm retired now, semi. Just look in on things now and then, straighten out the tangles, give the morale a lift and so forth."

Thursday swallowed another caustic reply. Kelly Dow might be a blabber-mouthed nuisance but he might also, someday, be a potential client. So Thursday said gravely, "That's the kind of job I'd like, Mr. Dow."

"You play your cards right in this Weaver business and you'll be able to retire too," said Dow. "He's got plenty of dough and he won't need it where he's going."

Ivah Hecht winced. He murmured, "Kelly, please."

"Bushwah," said Dow. "Weaver's got no more chance of beating this rap than I have of swimming the Channel. Less, come to think of it. I made a pretty fair showing in the rough water swim this year."

"A man's innocent until proved guilty," Hecht said wearily; the subject had apparently been discussed before Thursday's arrival.

"And I saw Weaver has convicted himself, right out of his own mouth. Even our stupid police department can see that."

"I thought you had connections there," Thursday commented.

"I'm in on the inside," Dow agreed. "I ought to be, after that Gifford girl case—you remember it, Thursday. I'm the one who found her body down that canyon. The police were running around in circles, of course."

"Of course."

"Too much politics, red tape, out-of-date routine. Always pussyfooting, not enough direct businesslike action." He scowled reflectively. "Good thing they nabbed Weaver in such short order. Never can tell what he'd have done if they hadn't. He might've run amuck or something."

Hecht shoved the oar-handles aside and got up suddenly. "That's enough for me," and Thursday wasn't certain whether he meant the exercise or the conversation. "You feel in the mood for a rubdown, Kelly?"

"Never had one yet and I don't intend to start now."

"Well, thanks for the lunch. Be sure to drop in any time you're near the office." Hecht took Thursday's arm and led him across the floor. When Thursday glanced back, Kelly Dow was commencing to row again energetically.

In a small pungent anteroom, a muscular young fellow in

white ducks and T-shirt lay on a rubbing table reading a physical culture magazine. "What's the good word, Mr. Hecht? Same old treatment?"

"Gus, you're about to make five dollars." The young man jumped to the floor grinning, caught the key Hecht tossed him. "Get the scotch from my locker and locate some setups. Then forget the rubdown for a while, understand?"

"The only thing I can remember is the five, Mr. Hecht."

The door closed behind Gus. Hecht tapped Thursday's arm apologetically. "Man, I'm sorry, but what could I do? Dow's a client, big account—and he did take me to lunch." With a twinkle, "And not at good old K-D Number One."

"What's this malarkey about police connections? Or was it malarkey?"

"Nine-tenths. The remaining tenth is that he did find that girl's body two-three years ago. Blind luck, true. It might've been the Boy Scouts or the National Guard, they were searching too. But it was Kelly who stumbled on it, out with his riding club, and he's fancied himself quite the detective ever since."

"Oh. I had half a notion you might be pulling some strings."

Hecht's twinkle faded away. He hoisted himself heavily onto the edge of the rubbing table and sat there gloomily digging his fingers into his plump knees. "I wish to heaven I could do that for Bliss. But for all his guff, Dow is discouragingly accurate. Bliss is in deep."

"I talked with Lieutenant Clapp."

"Then you know what I do, or more. Frankly, Thursday, the situation is beyond me. Bliss isn't telling the truth to the police or to me."

Cool relief flooded through Thursday. "Then you think he did it." If Weaver's own attorney believed him guilty . . .

"Absolutely not," said Hecht, looking surprised. "Do you?"

"You admit he isn't telling the truth," Thursday dodged the issue. "And there's his reputation for violence."

"What I should have said, he's not telling the whole truth.

48

Why Bliss should hold back anything in this crisis, I don't know." Merle *might* be the reason, Thursday's logic admitted grudgingly. Hecht was shaking his head slowly. "But as for killing Joyce, absolutely not. The boy's unusually chivalrous, though he was driven to striking her once when they were both in their cups. Have you seen the noon papers, by the way? They have him in the gas chamber already; the trial is a mere formality."

"At the moment that's the outlook, I'm afraid."

"I intend otherwise," said the plump little man fiercely. Then he beamed wistfully at Thursday. "I haven't told you how deeply I appreciate your change of heart. I need your experienced help."

"Don't mention it," Thursday muttered. He wasn't here to help Weaver, only to prove him guilty to his own satisfaction.

The door opened and Gus reappeared with drinking materials on a tray. After he'd gone again, Hecht held up the bottle questioningly but Thursday shook his head so Hecht said, "If you don't mind," and poured a stiff one for himself. Silence for a moment, the only sound the clink of ice cubes and the fizz of soda water and a gurgle in Hecht's throat. He sighed.

"Yes, women have always made a fool of Bliss. He's had bad luck, chosen badly, and his local prominence has made news of it." Hecht had already polished off his first drink and started building another. "And between ourselves, Thursday, since we're now in allegiance . . . I'm presuming a hundred will serve as retainer—it'll be in tomorrow morning's mail . . . I was saying, the papers haven't got hold of the worst tale of all yet. Pray they don't. There's an insanity angle."

Thursday whistled softly. Then, "Isn't that a forensic way out?"

"Unfortunately, no. An uncle by marriage, no blood relationship. This uncle slew his wife with a meat cleaver, then tried to decapitate himself, pretty ghastly. No possible bearing on Bliss's case, of course, but you can imagine what the papers could do with it."

"It couldn't be admitted as evidence."

"Man, let's not kid ourselves. Jury trials begin in the head-lines, no matter what the textbooks say. At this moment, I doubt if any lawyer on earth could prove Bliss innocent. Our alternative is to prove someone else guilty—or at least to drag in enough red herring to create a reasonable doubt."

With the inclusive "our," Thursday realized clearly for the first time that he had been hired. Hecht was again mentioning his heartfelt appreciation and offering another drink and somewhere along the line Thursday had been hired to save Bliss Weaver. He had turned down Merle, whom he loved, but he had succumbed to this soft pink attorney he'd met but a few minutes before. "Red herring," said Thursday wonder-ingly and lit a cigar as if that might straighten out his mind. Was this what he had intended all along?

Hecht smiled over his glass. "Though it's only fair to warn you that I don't have Idea One where to start. You're the crim-inally experienced one."

"Oh, I think we're even up." Thursday began to walk around the massage room, puffing smoke and frowning at the towels and bottles. He remembered Clapp's angry order to steer clear from now on. He wondered whether Hecht, drink-ing comfortably on the rubbing table, was awfully adroit or awfully trusting. And he thought until something came. "Try this on for size. Plenty of holes in it, though."

"Never mind that."

"Joyce Shafto played the horses. She was short of cash, in debt, pawning things. Maybe she owed a potful to some bookie, welshed on it and the bookie killed her."

Hecht said doubtfully, "Hmm."

"Well, it's a red herring even if it does smell."

For some reason Hecht wasn't interested in the bookie angle. He said, "My thoughts were running more along crime-of-passion lines. Another man, jealousy, a lover's quar-rel—that sort of thing."

"You begin to fool with that angle and you're tailoring a

coat that'll fit Weaver as well," Thursday warned. "What you want is something that has nothing to do with Weaver. Between the two ideas, I'll vote for the bookie setup as the least dangerous."

Hecht huddled his fat shoulders uneasily. "Mine isn't a complete shot in the dark, I must confess. There's a fair chance there was another man. Remember, of course, that my acquaintance with Joyce Shafto was completely tenuous, first as my client's wife and then as my client's legal opponent. As to the divorce fight, my real contact was with her attorneys, Jeter & Burke."

"And *they* told you there was another man involved?"

"Good heavens, no! They have an impeccable reputation." Hecht fumbled for words. Thursday eyed him more closely, debating what could be bothering the congenitally jolly little man. Something more than worry for his client, obviously. "But I have heard a rumor in my circle—I can't tell you the source, very hush-hush—about Joyce Shafto and another man. She had correspondence from him, I understand. I was told that she kept a certain letter from him folded up in her compact."

"In her compact?" Thursday repeated in disbelief.

"I've heard of that habit of Joyce Shafto's before," Hecht assured him, "keeping her secrets in her compact. She used to carry an extra-large one for just that purpose. It's about five inches across, a gold or gold-colored octagonal, with a dragon on the outside." He hesitated. "I was thinking if you could get access to her things you might find the compact. We could that way get a line on the man." Perspiration beaded his bald spot as it beaded the glass he held.

"Sounds like the long way home to me." Thursday puffed at his cigar vigorously. "Discovering that Joyce had a certain boy friend doesn't prove anything one way or another. But we *know* she plunged on the ponies. We *know* she was short of cash. Seems to me there's a foundation to build on. Where would somebody who lived at Marcliff be likely to place bets?"

"I haven't the faintest idea," said Hecht vaguely and half-turned away to put ice cubes in his freshly empty glass "That's the sort of thing I wouldn't know." The first ice cube slipped to the floor but he made it with the next two. "Possibly something along that line might be in the compact. If you'd only find that . . ."

The dragon compact again; not necessarily the mysterious letter inside, but the compact itself. Hecht was clinging stubbornly to his one idea. Thursday shrugged, certain that the attorney—like his jailed client—wasn't telling everything he knew. "I'll think about it. And you reconsider the bookie angle. If you can't reach me at my office, leave a message. Or I'll phone you."

They shook hands and Hecht wished him good hunting with a little of his early joviality. But when Thursday looked back from the door, the attorney was pouring more almost-straight whisky into his red frightened face.

On his way out Thursday caught a glimpse of Kelly Dow ahead of him, also leaving. Dow was fully dressed now, swaggering along in a fringed leather jacket and a white sun helmet. He didn't see Thursday and Thursday kept it that way.

A short drive away, the corridors of police headquarters welcomed him with stony coldness. Clapp wasn't in, nor was Crane; the homicide detail was home catching up on lost sleep. Thursday looked in the press room, half-expecting to see Merle, but there was a male stranger's face at her familiar desk. Headlines read EARLY TRIAL HINTED IN WEAVER STRANGLING.

The city jail officer gave Thursday a cordial no. "Nobody's seeing Weaver except his lawyer. That's Weaver's idea as well as ours."

Thursday evaded stating his business and ambled back down the corridor to the vice squad's office. Lieutenant Richards, the squad chief, was drowsing through a boring stack of non-local FBI surveys. He was glad to be interrupted by Thursday's studiously idle call. "What's the handbook situation around and about, Rick?"

"We shut 'em up as fast as we find 'em. Thinking of opening a drop?"

"Maybe. Where'd you advise? I hear business is good in La Jolla."

"Then get the wax out of your ears. La Jolla's as clean as a whistle."

And that was that. Thursday fooled away another hour talking to the cops he knew, guiding the conversation obliquely toward Bliss Weaver and Joyce Shafto. He learned nothing new. At three o'clock he drove into the sweltering center of town and sat in the reception room of Jeter & Burke, Attorneys-at-Law, until the senior partner was available. All he learned there was that the firm had no desire to discuss their clients, particularly dead ones.

And so, at four o'clock he returned to his own office, frustrated and empty of ideas. The mail was routine. Routinely, he checked in with Telephone Secretarial Service. And there was a single call for him: Ivah Hecht.

Hecht answered his office phone personally but his voice was so blurred that Thursday didn't recognize him immediately. "Say, man, thought it over. Thought it over from end to end. Something I got to tell you but don't tell I told you." Thursday realized then that Hecht was completely, stupidly drunk.

"I'm listening, Mr. Hecht. What have you decided to tell me?"

"Another rumor I remembered. Very hush-hush source, you understand that, man." Hecht giggled. "She did have a bookie. House of Buena, that's where. Funny old name, huh? It was her beauty parlor—what do you think of that?"

Abruptly, Hecht hung up. After a moment Thursday did the same, wondering why Hecht had to get drunk to tell him.

CHAPTER 9

He wandered by the place twice, studying it. The flat front of the House of Buena yearned for attention amid all the drab flat-fronted shops of upper Broadway. Its facade was frosted with dark green stucco, and fancy white ironwork criss-crossed the windows and a white iron grill gate made the entrance important. The shop's name appeared only on a bronze shield bolted to the gate, along with hours of business and the news that it catered to ladies only. For a beauty parlor or a bookie shop it looked conspicuously bizarre.

While Thursday loitered, a pair of patrons departed, well-groomed women, handsomely dressed. He was pleased. Above all, a society bookie wouldn't want the slightest disturbance, not with the better-class clientele. Ignoring the ladies-only sign, Thursday went in; he was confident now that he could get the information he was after, even if it meant twisting an arm or two.

Within was more white ironwork and an atmosphere of perfumed velvet. Dainty green palms in marble jardinières nodded their spiky fronds under the caress of the air-cooling system. He had entered a waiting room. In rooms on either side he could see women in starched white who tended other women subjected to various gleaming machines. Before him a carpeted ramp ascended to a grilled mezzanine at the rear.

He could feel the three women in the waiting room eye him with covert suspicion. From the left advanced an older woman, without a gray hair out of place, to inquire if she could help him.

In a voice deliberately loud, he announced, "I'm here to see Mr. Buena. I don't want to be put off." All around, glances raised from magazines and knitting.

Nothing disturbed the gray-haired woman's polite smile.

"I'm afraid there is no Mr. Buena," she said. "If you—"

"Never mind that," Thursday cut her off. "Let me see the boss, no matter who he is now."

The rudeness was for effect, to soften up those who feared police tactics, and it began to tell on the woman. She flushed, stammering, "Well—I don't—"

She was interrupted again. From the shadows on the iron-grilled mezzanine an ice-cold voice said, "Tell the *gentleman* to come up if he wishes to see me."

Thursday looked up. His bright ideas about arm-twisting collapsed into foolish wreckage. For the person who sat at the top of the ramp, regarding him hostilely, was a young woman in a wheelchair.

Overly conscious of all the feminine eyes watching, he marched up the ramp. He had chosen his gambit and now he had to play it out. But, on the mezzanine, he played it in a quieter voice. "You the boss here?"

"Yes, I'm Buena Echavez. What did you want?"

"Police business."

She looked him over, her eyes black velvet flecked with frost. She spun her lightweight chromed wheelchair around deftly, tossed "Come in here then," at him like a bone, and rolled away. He followed, chuckling inside at the way she'd taken the lead away from him.

The second door in the short dead-end hall was a large combination bedroom and sitting room, grandly and massively furnished in mahogany. It was warmer here upstairs and in this humid jungle air flourished a number of potted growths, philodendron, rubber plants, dwarf palms, and begonias in hanging baskets. Through a half-open door toward the front he could glimpse the office he had anticipated. Buena Echavez parked by the four-poster bed, her back to the rear wall where tapestries hid probable windows.

There were no chairs since she had no use for them, nor did she ask him to sit down at all. She inquired acidly, "What's this about police business, Mr. Thursday?"

He studied her with grim deliberation then, getting a little angered that she could stay so far ahead of him. She had no business being a woman, a cripple, or aware of his unofficial status. How did she know him? "Nice to be expected," he said.

In contrast to her cold eyes and voice, she had a warm ripe mouth which curled into a fleeting smile at his remark. Analyzing her, reaching for his next move, he felt a general regret that such a potentially striking woman should be condemned to a helpless existence on chrome wheels. Her too-slim unusable legs were locked in silver-colored braces that matched the silver rosette ornaments on her black frock. Her voice bore no hint of accent; only her name and her most handsome features—the fine aquiline nose, the glossy black hair bunned in back—told of her Mexican descent. Much was green in the room, giving her flesh an exotic greenish-golden tinge. Her firm bare arms looked loving; within her frock the smooth flesh swelled splendidly into proud slow-moving breasts—but it was impossible to forget her bondage.

She haughtily waited until the end of his inspection, then plucked a red camellia from a shrub near the head of her bed and fastened it in her hair. "Will that serve as a distraction?" she asked expressionlessly.

"I don't remember complaining."

"Call it a form of chivalry, then. A woman should be at her best when entertaining in the bedroom."

She was mocking him with her infirmity. "I didn't come for entertainment, young lady. I do happen to be working with the cops for the time being."

She coolly mouthed a foul word in Spanish, then repeated it in English so he wouldn't miss it.

Thursday snorted. "You try too hard to shock, kid. Easy on my weak heart, will you?" He laughed at her and made himself at home on the edge of her huge bed. "A real high-class bookie behaves nicer."

He expected denial or a smoke screen of anger. Instead she

fooled him again with the fleeting smile. Despite her youth, faint crow's-feet lined the corners of her eyes. "Now shall I swoon?" she asked.

"Now shall you talk about Joyce Shafto? Or are you going to deny you ever knew her?"

"Have I denied anything yet? Please don't get worked up, Mr. Thursday."

"Like every other sucker, Joyce Shafto lost on the horses. She was head over heels in debt. Now she's dead."

"I subscribe to three newspapers. Her husband did it, didn't he?"

"She was in debt to you. Since gambling debts aren't legally binding in this state, there's only one way to make a deadbeat pay up and that's to threaten. If you threaten, you've got to follow through. The result is a dead deadbeat."

This time she laughed, scornfully, and flipped a finger against her braces, causing a musical ringing sound. "And how did I do it?"

"No. How did you have it done?"

From the adjoining office a flat voice said, "Miss Buena . . ." Thursday swung around quickly but it was only the intercom on the desk. Buena wheeled her chair past the door, not bothering to close it, and flipped a switch and spoke into the box. The downstairs woman's voice said, "Mrs. Moore would like to come up to pay her respects."

"Ask her to wait a few moments, please." Then Buena rolled back to face Thursday again. "You were saying?"

"To pay her respects?" Thursday inquired. "Or to collect on the fourth at Tanforan?"

"Oh, don't harp," said Buena, making a point of looking sleepy. "If you're a blue-nose about off-track betting, you're in the wrong place. If you're hunting something more sinister, you're in an even wronger place. So good day."

"I'm hunting information about Joyce Shafto. You give it to me and we'll part friends."

"That really wouldn't be possible no matter what I gave

you. Look, I'll admit I couldn't set a spit-curl without a book of directions. Yet I'm not in the least frightened because you know that. You couldn't prove anything even if you wanted to—which I don't think you do."

"Don't be too sure what I want. I might surprise you, young lady."

"I sincerely doubt that. You're not greatly subtle and you're not greatly clever, swaggering in here at the top of your lungs. No, as a bully or as a brain, you don't scare me at all, Mr. Thursday. I'm sorry—but you just don't."

Thursday got off her bed. In a gentler voice, he said, "And I'm sorry too. You're due an apology for the way I acted. I'm making it."

For the first time, Buena Echavez seemed a trifle off-balance. Her smile came on broadly and it stayed on. "So I was wrong—you can surprise me." With the frost still in her eyes, "But I'm not wrong about the other. I'm so safe that you can't touch me, Mr. Thursday."

"All I want is to know about Joyce Shafto. What I want I usually get."

"How very comforting that must be," she said, with a brief glance downward at her braces. "Now, if you'll excuse me, I have a customer waiting."

It was both deadlock and challenge. Going down the ramp, Thursday passed a pearl-hung middle-aged woman going up. Politely he said, "Afternoon, Mrs. Moore," and got a surprised smile in return.

Out in the sultry late afternoon, he circled around the block to the alley and walked down it, staring up at the back of the House of Buena. A steel fire-escape stairway angled up the rear wall to a covered porch on the second floor. It was easy to figure that a door opened somewhere through the wall that was obscured by tapestries in Buena's room. But he wondered who used that stairway and probable door—other bettors? He doubted it, from his estimation of her clientele; they weren't back-way people. Yet Buena Echavez would have no use for such an exit or entrance.

His office was within walking distance. He hurried there and got to work on her. His professional pride was ruffled by the invulnerability she claimed. But when, an hour later, he replaced the telephone receiver for the final time, he scowled at his notes. He knew who she was and where she came from. Local, fourth generation American, an only child of divorced parents, an ambitious inflexible girl who had worked her way through college as a theater usherette, waitress, carhop, bank messenger. An economics major at San Diego State, a phenomenal scholastic record—the professor to whom Thursday talked had had much to say about Buena's potentialities in the commercial field. "One of the few I can honestly say learned everything I presented. She could have taught the course herself, afterward, except for matters of considered judgment which, of course, will come with age. A dirty shame, that poliomyelitis. Do you happen to know what she's doing now?" Then after the illness, an utterly blank year. Two years ago she had opened the House of Buena as a high-priced beautician.

Lieutenant Richards couldn't help. "No, there aren't any drops in that neighborhood that I know of. If you've got a line, give me the word."

"No, nothing now, Rick. Just checking an angle."

And Thursday grimaced as he slouched in his darkening office. No betting slips had been found in Joyce Shafto's apartment. Thursday wasn't, as Buena had suggested, a blue-nose about off-track betting, but he did long for a weapon to hold over her head. Frozen in that chair-bound cake of ice was some information he wanted, he was sure of that. But, now understanding the methods of Buena Echavez, he couldn't conceive of any threat that might crack her open. She *was* invulnerable to police tactics. At the moment, Buena seemed absolutely right. He couldn't touch her.

CHAPTER 10

After a dawdling bemused dinner in a restaurant's rear booth, he returned to Marcliff, his fourth journey there in twenty-four hours. He had some vague notion of steeping himself in Joyce Shafto's life—and he had nowhere else to go. He had no way to pressure Buena Echavez. Ivah Hecht's drunken information wasn't enough, and Thursday was positive the attorney moved in a fog of half-truths anyway. A recent memory of Hecht's rosy haunted face; he might be afraid for his life. Certainly he was gnawed by a fear greater than that of attorney for client.

But how could Thursday dispel that gray barrier of lies? He didn't dare try. If he made an enemy of Hecht, he would lose his single legal entrance to the case. He needed that front doorway; he had a professional reputation to uphold, and he knew better than to try to outfox Clapp. Thursday's mouth bent in a pained smile. Only this morning he had fought tooth and nail to keep out of the Weaver case.

The lower floor of Joyce Shafto's wing glowed with windows of light. Above, only the foyer lamps burned dimly. The dead woman's name had already been removed from above her mailbox. Of the three remaining names (of which the other second-story tenants were vacationing happily distant) Thursday chose the handiest, Folk.

Mr. Folk answered his ring, a mildly petulant face with thin hair and thick bifocals. Thursday introduced himself into their fruit-wood provincial surroundings and Mrs. Folk, flapping in the background, pounced upon the conversation. The husband faded back to tinkering with the television set muttering warnings to himself about high voltage. Mrs. Folk, gaunt and relentless, pressed a cup of tea on Thursday, cornered him in a chair and Told All.

Except that Bliss Weaver had long been suspected in this household of being a dangerous fiend, he learned only one thing he didn't already know. And that displeased him: the evening papers were already publicizing Max Thursday as working on the Weaver case. It wouldn't make his job any easier and it was certain to annoy Clapp.

The only discrepancy he noticed was that the Folks placed Bliss Weaver in the apartment above for a considerably longer period than his own observation had. But witnesses' time evaluations were seldom dependable.

He finally escaped with an "official business" excuse and crossed the foyer to ring the bell whose card read Miss Nancy Quinlan in a spidery scrawl.

But the dumpy little spinster wouldn't admit him. Her pale biscuit-face eyed him apprehensively and she twitched nervously at her lace collar and cuffs. Only Thursday's gruff mention of police authority let him continue his interview through the narrow slot of a door secured by a night-chain.

"Forgive my premonitions," she said in her dry whisper. "But it might have been me instead last night—do you understand? They say it was her husband but I know better than that."

Thursday felt a leap of interest. "I don't think it was her husband either."

"No, no, you wouldn't understand. You're too material. You haven't *seen* him as I have."

"Perhaps I have." His heart was tapping out victorious hopes now.

"Thin—little—with that terrible scar across his mouth? No, you couldn't possibly have seen him watching because it's only myself he watches. Myself, he's waiting to catch. I've sometimes hidden from him, in the house, in the closet. Then he goes away until later."

Thursday's heart returned to normal. No wonder Crane had ruled Nancy Quinlan out as a witness; a persecution complex was probably the least of her harmless delusions.

A powdery wrinkled hand seized his as he was saying good-bye and turning away. "Not just around the grounds, but in dreams. I leave all the lights on but he still comes for me, in different forms. Last night he rang my doorbell and rang and rang. I was going to give up and let him in, but then I woke up and he went away. I heard him clanking up the stairs. I knew then that something horrible was about to happen. And didn't it?"

Although reasonably material, Thursday felt the chill snaking up his spine. He disengaged his hand from the cold old one. "I'll keep an eye out for him."

"It won't do any good," Nancy Quinlan said hopelessly. "Everyone's turn comes round." She closed the door, locking it.

Thursday sat down on the front steps and lit a cigar to restore the earthbound feeling. "Clanking up the stairs," he muttered. He smiled feebly at the dark muted ocean. After a long thoughtful while, he went in search of the administration office. The superintendent was sucking his tongue over first-of-the-month entries in a fat ledger. Thursday was braced for an argument but the superintendent had seen him leave that morning with Lieutenant Clapp. He surrendered the key to the Shafto apartment without question.

So once again Thursday stood on the rush matting in the deathly silent apartment and gazed around at the gray crouching furniture. For the first time here, he was completely alone and he could feel it. He was not without imagination. He prowled cautiously into the bedroom, found himself listening for sounds without knowing what sounds he might expect. The slow liquid drum-drum of the surf, a gay thin laugh from the beach, everything normal and still he felt uneasy. Aware, as if on the verge of some grim momentous discovery.

He snickered at his tenseness. "Waiting for advice from the dead woman?" he murmured, and his voice sounded shockingly loud.

He commenced a search. He went about it conscientiously, turning back the blankets on the bed, moving furniture, raising the rugs, examining the undersides of drawers. He found only the miscellaneous accretion of everyday living: stray pins and crumpled paper handkerchiefs and forgotten receipts. But he found not a single betting slip, no souvenir of any long-shot that had finished disastrously yet comically out of the money. He kept at it, though, thinking (as Joyce Shafto must often have thought) Better Luck Next Time. He brooded his way through a vanity crammed with feminine paraphernalia, lipsticks and bottles of guaranteed beauty, and metal gadgets whose cosmetic function he wasn't sure of. He uncovered compacts too, but none that were octagonal with a dragon on the lid.

He sat down on the bed and read through Joyce Shafto's correspondence without curiosity. Most of the letters she'd kept were from her attorneys, reporting on the progress of her war against her husband, asking her please to call. There were a few desultory letters from her older sister Polly, a fabric wholesaler in Akron, Ohio, careless mentions of a buying trip to California "sometime" when they must surely see each other again. Nothing cordial, and the offhand "sometime" was far too late for Joyce now. Certain letters from men whose names meant nothing to Thursday could scarcely be classified as love letters.

And none of the letters—even conceivably important communiques from her attorneys—had ever been folded to fit in the largest of compacts. Hecht had either been mistaken about that peculiar trait or he had lied. And if he had lied—why?

Back in the living room again Thursday examined the dark smudge on the woven rug by the door. A little more than an inch across, it looked to him about like the stains seen on mechanics' overalls. On his hands and knees, he rubbed a little of the smear onto his handkerchief with a half-urge to get it analyzed at his own expense. But he knew on second thought that Clapp had already done that. The homicide chief hardly ever missed. Thursday crept around the apartment looking for other similar stains. He found none.

The kitchen was still in cozy disarray, a dirty dish and glass on the tile drainboard, the gutted can of tamales in the trash, the pan on the stove ringed with red sauce. Thursday leaned against the stove and tried to pin down an errant sense of loss: that something was missing from the night before. Joyce's body, of course, but something else—a sound, a smell, an impression—had changed. He watched the pilot flame burn its calm vigil and wondered when the utilities would be turned off.

And suddenly he straightened, staring hard at the little gas flame. He left the apartment hurriedly and trotted down the steps and outside. There he stopped and faced the building again.

Like an actor rehearsing a sure-fire bit of business he walked slowly back into the downstairs foyer. He halted in front of Miss Nancy Quinlan's fear-locked door and pretended to ring the bell several times. Then he turned for the stairs. Halfway up them, he paused to take a deep experimental breath.

That was the difference—*the air.* Last night it had held the unmistakable taint of escaped gas. Tonight it didn't.

A smile began to harden on his mouth, growing. He continued his climb to the second floor, whispering like a child at play, "Clank—clank—clank—" He repeated his pantomime in front of Joyce Shafto's door, pretending to ring the bell, waiting.

But this door he entered, smiling at the ghost of Joyce Shafto, and as he entered he made-believe to set something down just inside the door. And found he had put his invisible burden down directly on the grease smudge.

"Oh, I got it, I got it," he breathed, and his smile spread into a grin, the first real grin he'd had all day.

CHAPTER 11

Thursday rapped lightly on the H in Homicide. Beyond the door, Clapp growled and Thursday let himself in. The big lieutenant was slouched grumpily behind his littered desk, tapping rhythms on it with a yellow pencil. "Your wife told me you were still here," Thursday said. "She also told me to remind you it's nearly eleven and if your watch is broken—" He broke off his light pave-the-way patter at the sight of Merle.

She wore the same severely tailored dress as when she had awakened him that morning. The long day's wear told on her dress and on her haggard face. She sat stiffly upright on a straight chair in one drab corner of the office, raw effort in every line of her body.

Thursday's surprised reflex came out as, "What're you doing here, honey?" The endearment was a cruel accident. He hoped it had gotten lost in the low-pitched mutter of the police radio that filled and depressed the room with its almost indistinguishable monotony.

"How do you expect me to stay away?" she answered wearily, and looked at the floor rather than at him.

Clapp said harshly, "Let's turn it around—what are *you* doing here?"

"Ivah Hecht hired me to help him, Clapp. I'm working for Weaver."

"Indeed? He must pay real well."

Thursday caught his eyes, cold as bullet ends. "Not so much. Look, this morning you said I had to make up for something. Are you going to give me a fair try at it? I've got a legal right to investigate but I'm in no position to fight the police department."

Clapp's eyes bored deep into his, reading him. "What I said

65

this morning, son, was that you never could make up for it."

"I'll try." Thursday glanced anxiously at Merle. "I suppose she knows about the handkerchief."

"I know," she murmured, not looking at him. "I'm too sick with this whole business to think it's very important."

"I do." Clapp shoved a *Sentinel* pink sheet across his desk. It rattled, moving toward Thursday. "This your work, Max?"

WEAVER HOMICIDAL MANIAC?

Thursday stiffened over the headline. Spread double columned down the center of the front page was the story about Bliss Weaver's uncle, the insanity angle. It skirted libel in the sword-dancing *Sentinel* style. How had they picked up the tale so quickly? Thursday's mind flashed to Ivah Hecht, his telephone voice babbling out information he had held back while sober.

"I'll admit I deserve that crack," Thursday said slowly. "But it didn't come from me."

"I wonder. I notice you're parading yourself through tonight's papers as taking on the Weaver case. What's tomorrow's scoop— your true confessions about Merle?"

Thursday flinched, then flared up. "None of that's mine. Listen, big shot—" He got a grip on himself. "Sorry, Clapp."

"Yeh. Me too."

"I came in here to prove you something. Bliss Weaver isn't guilty."

Merle's eyes flashed up, wide and unbelieving. Clapp leaned back and let out a sigh that mingled with the drone of the radio ordering Car 12 to investigate a disturbance at a skating rink. Merle's gaze clung dumbly to Thursday as she turned down the radio a little. Watching her, Clapp growled reluctantly, "Okay, speak your piece. Weave your magic spell."

Thursday licked his lips, frowned at his shoes, reaching for

66

the suddenly elusive arguments of his reconstruction. He had recited it a dozen times in his mind, but now at the crucial moment . . . "Joyce Shafto was killed just a few minutes before Weaver—and I—arrived," he began. "We both barely missed seeing the murderer leave the building. The person who strangled her didn't intend to kill her, just meant to shut her up or scare her. All the murderer intended to do was rob her. That's who your killer really is, Clapp—an apartment prowler."

No reaction from Clapp. Thursday said, "I've learned there's been a man watching Marcliff for the past week or so, a thin guy with a badly scarred mouth, casing the place for a burglary. I figure he specializes in rich single women and that particular building was ideal pickings—secluded and with two unprotected women, Joyce and the Quinlan woman, both apparently wealthy. Of course, Joyce wasn't, but no doubt she put on a good front."

"About this man watching the apartment," Clapp remarked idly. "You got that from Miss Quinlan?"

"That's right."

"Uh-huh. Disregarding the fact that she's senile, is a budding paranoiac, is a devotee of spirit circles—"

"Disregarding all that," Thursday said doggedly. "On the night of the murder—in fact, as the opening event of the murder—somebody rang her doorbell. When she didn't answer, the same somebody went on upstairs, making a clanking noise."

"You also want to disregard the fact that she was asleep or half-asleep when this happened and probably dreamed the whole thing?"

"Go along with me for a minute, just for the sake of the argument," Thursday pleaded, and the homicide chief folded his hands indifferently. "I say this. Scarmouth wears those blue chalk-stripe overalls like a Gas & Electric Company repairman. He carried a metal tool kit as part of his act. He came into the building, saw that the Quinlan woman's lights were on (not knowing that she leaves them on all night) and rang her bell. He got no answer but he did wake Nancy Quinlan up. And it was the metal tool kit she heard clanking as he kept going up the stairs to Joyce's place. He rang the bell there, gave her his line about a gas leak, she let him in—"

Clapp groaned. "What woman living alone is going to admit a scarface character at that time of night, even with gas company overalls?"

"Scarmouth has a clincher. This is the modus operandi I've read about somewhere, a pressure spray device like one of those insecticide bombs, uh, aerosol. Only this gadget is filled with natural gas. As Joyce comes to open the door, Scarmouth uses this push-button spray. She smells the gas, it scares her and makes Scarmouth look genuine, and so she opens up." Thursday paused, then said emphatically, "And when I went up there a few minutes after Weaver—I could still smell the gas."

"Boy, do you kill me," Clapp murmured. "I read the Quinlan evidence too and you're leaving out a slight detail. Scarmouth is supposed to be a thin little guy. The hands that bruised Joyce Shafto's neck didn't belong to any little guy."

"I haven't got the whole thing taped," Thursday said lamely. "Let me finish. As soon as Joyce let Scarmouth in, he set his dirty tool kit down on the carpet just inside the door. That accounts for the grease mark. Then he tried to scare Joyce into submission while he started a search for valuables, which accounts for the two open drawers. But she made a break for it, he grabbed her—"

"Neat. And why did Joyce dress up in her evening gown? You account for everything except the case we have against Weaver." Clapp grimaced, a sidelong apologetic glance toward Merle, who was watching Thursday fixedly, afraid or too tired to let hope show. "Thursday, it's not that I want to send Weaver over. But have you forgotten that Weaver swears he left Joyce alive? And that much more reliable witnesses—I mean Mr. and Mrs. Folk—give him thirty minutes with her?"

"I'm a more reliable witness than the Folks and I say only ten," Thursday argued. "They're figuring from the time *Scarmouth*, not Weaver, rang Joyce's doorbell. As for Weaver, he spent his ten minutes in shock, staring at his wife's body, which he found dead and left the same way. Weaver made up his lies for the D. A. because of some farfetched ideas about protecting Merle. Because he knows he didn't kill Joyce, he can't believe anybody else will actually think he did."

During a long silence, Thursday knew he had failed. Merle still sat in her corner chair, pale and withdrawn. She hadn't even wearily clutched at his straw. Clapp too was detached, playing with the pencil again, but when he spoke it was in a kindlier tone. "Maybe I know somewhat how you feel, Max. A conscience is a heck of a thing to have, isn't it? But your case doesn't jell."

"All right, maybe my guilty conscience did start me thinking. But that doesn't necessarily make my case wrong. Weaver didn't kill that woman." Frustrated, Thursday whirled to Merle. "Why don't you say something? At least *you* believe he's innocent."

She said slowly, "I don't know."

He was staring at her, dumfounded, when Clapp snapped, "Turn that radio up!"

". . . homicide. Car 23 reports body young woman at 8th Avenue, G Street, apparently strangled. Notify all . . . "

As if it had been an overdue signal, Clapp sprang for his hat. "Well, there's number two."

Thursday rounded the desk to block his departure. "This might be it, maybe the clincher. If this one is like the Shafto strangling, Weaver is in the clear."

Clapp scowled blankly. "What on earth are you talking about?"

Merle understood first and her gasp was like a sob. "Clapp—*he doesn't know!*"

Thursday tried to look at them both at once. Clapp said heavily, "Bliss Weaver broke loose. He's been running loose since sundown."

CHAPTER 12

Clapp touched the siren button and everything on Market Street veered out of his path. Inside the police sedan as it rushed with a howl through the warm midnight was one of the few breezes in town. Thursday held onto his hat, and Merle, a silent passenger in the back seat, guarded her hair with her hands.

"How'd you miss hearing it on the radio?" Clapp asked loudly. "My department's taking the rap for this one. Crane and Pensic—you know him, chief of detectives—were transporting Weaver from city jail uptown to county jail. The arraignment's tomorrow, at least it *was*. Freak accident—blasted cab driver didn't stop at an intersection, ran smack into the squad car. Crane got knocked silly against the windshield. So Weaver socks Pensic in the eye and makes a break."

Thursday couldn't quite absorb the idea of Weaver's escape. "No cuffs?"

Clapp swore at the world blurring by. "No, no cuffs. Weaver had been docile—and he does have a certain standing in the community. . . . Makes us look pretty efficient, huh? Worse'n that now there's a second one." Through gritted, hard-grinning teeth, "So let's have no more bilge about Weaver being a poor misunderstood boy, huh?"

Thursday grabbed the dashboard as the sedan squealed around the 8th Avenue corner. "Sorry about the spot you're in, Clapp." He was; and he couldn't humanly expect the harassed detective-lieutenant to go for his specious reconstruction of Weaver's innocence now. "Crane all right?"

"Yeah, he's out prowling for the escapee now. So's Pensic—that big ox didn't appreciate getting slugged much. Don't worry, we'll get our boy."

A motorcycle cop waved them through a midblock cluster

70

of peering faces and they rolled on to the G Street intersection, where Clapp parked. He said to Merle, "You wait. You got enough on your mind." When Thursday asked permission to tag along, Clapp growled, "Oh, I'm sure the press will expect you." Then he half-grinned to indicate he only half meant it.

Thursday suddenly laughed. "Okay, I'll be your whipping boy. *I* didn't lose Weaver."

For an instant Clapp looked mad enough to fight. Then he chuckled himself, said, "It's a big world and a long life," and strode almost cheerfully toward the murder.

ORIGINAL RANCHERS MARKET—Market Days Wednesday & Saturday. Blue-lettered orange signs, almost identical in dilapidation, faced both streets. The place was nothing more, not a tourist attraction nor smugly picturesque in any way. A right-angle of sheet-iron booths, fronting the broad sidewalks for a half block on each street, the Ranchers Market corner provided a retail location for those local farmers who might wish to sell their produce at their own prices. The gloomy stalls gaped emptily at the street, open from the front save for a low continuous counter. Behind was an asphalt parking lot. Flashlights wandered everywhere in the dark.

Clapp and Thursday headed for a G Street booth lit shadowly by a prowl car spotlight. A plainclothes detective named Bryan trotted hurriedly to meet them; he had recently been transferred to Clapp's detail after a long wait and he was anxious to please. But all his greeting got was a grunt and a, "Well, where is she?"

"Lieutenant—she's in the icebox!"

Clapp vaulted over the ancient counter. "Let me have a look, do you mind?" Broad uniformed shoulders got out of his way. Clapp took Bryan's flashlight, and he and Thursday gazed down into the box. It was a ramshackle wooden cooler in which countless cakes of ice had melted, giving its blackened plank sides a moldering secretive look. Clapp experimentally closed the rickety lid of the makeshift cooler. With the lid down, it looked more than ever like an over-size coffin. "Put out those cigarettes and get to work," Clapp said, and a minute later he and Thursday were alone in the booth. He tilted back the cooler lid and they silently inspected the dead girl.

She was a young brunette, far younger than Joyce Shafto, with blunt plain features; she had never been as pretty as Joyce Shafto. Yet there was an unmistakable resemblance between the two: the purplish agonized face and the mottled neck where big hands had squeezed. She huddled on her side, as if sleeping with her dark eyes bulged open, on the dry bottom of the box.

"Identification?" asked Clapp. "Hey, Bryan!"

"Haven't got it yet," Bryan said, hurrying back. "She's Mexican from the look of her. That might mean Mexican national or it might not. No purse." He added with an attempt at humor, "And she ain't talking."

Clapp just gave him another grunt. "Who found her? And how?"

"Out back here." Bryan swung open the stall's rear door—more sheet metal reinforced with angle-iron—and led them out onto the asphalt parking lot, hidden from both streets. A dusty battered GMC truck sat in the center of the lot, crates of tomatoes lashed perilously high on its bed. Seated on its running board were two stolid-faced overalled Japanese with beseeching eyes. "They rent this stand. Came up from Otay tonight, figured on catching forty winks in the truck and be ready to move their tomatoes in the morning. Father and son."

"Hold them. I'll want to talk to them presently."

As Bryan moved away, Thursday murmured, "You notice her feet?" and Clapp nodded. They went back inside. Clapp swept the light around on the concrete floor, discovered nothing. He cast the glow on the Mexican girl again. She was dressed in cheap pink taffeta, possibly the grandest clothes she owned. Thursday said, "No stockings, that's not unusual in this weather—but where's her shoes?"

Clapp summoned another detective and gave him general

orders for a more intensive search. Thursday had bent into the cooler and was examining the girl's bare feet. He called up, "Hey, here's a funny one."

"Get your head out of that box. You sound like a voice from the grave."

"Marks on her heels look like she was dragged in here barefoot, over the asphalt out back. Meaning she was already dead or close to it. She's still warm. Your boys looking for footprints?"

"Sure. Not much chance on that surface." Clapp asked a passing shadow if Doc Stein had shown up yet; he wanted a time of death.

"No purse and no shoes," Thursday mused, standing up. "Does that make sense to you?"

"Plenty. There's no purse because she was killed for her money, probably grabbed out on the sidewalk and dragged in here. Maybe through the auto entrance on 8th or the one on G. Bliss Weaver was broke when he escaped—he needs money to live, to get away." Clapp paused, shrugged. "Go-money, I think was his wife's pet phrase. It's plenty apt now."

"I can't see Weaver—"

"Sure you can. You ever been broke and running? Look at those marks on the poor kid's neck. The angle—I'll bet it's broken."

"Well, did Weaver need her shoes too?"

"They'll turn up," Clapp promised coolly. But they hadn't yet.

"You know what just occurred to me? Joyce was missing her purse too. I mean, she had plenty of pocketbooks around her apartment but not the one she was currently using. You know how women do—transfer their billfolds and identification and junk from one purse to another, whichever one they're carrying. That's the purse that was missing from her apartment."

"I see. We'll discuss later about going through that apartment without authorization," Clapp said. "Meanwhile that purse idea is as lousy as the others you've been having. Joyce was hard up, she had no money. She didn't drive a car so she didn't have a license. She didn't work so she didn't have a social security card. What billfold, son? Why'd she need one? Any one of her purses was as current as another."

"I just thought it might have been stolen too," Thursday said mildly. "Just trying to see a pattern."

"Steal an empty purse?" Clapp said mockingly. "I thought you were trying to sell me an apartment prowler. Now it's a purse snatcher. Forget it, Max, forget about patterns. This is just another plain crazy murder."

Thursday looked at him. "You're beginning to talk like the *Sentinel*."

"My job's to catch him, not analyze him. No, there's no blood tie-up between Weaver and that uncle of his. On the other hand, that's no proof that Weaver can't slip his cable independently. Think over what you know about him, volatile, unpredictable—"

"Sounds to my ears like the police could stand a little help," said a man's hearty voice behind them. Clapp swung his flashlight around quickly to illuminate a white sun helmet and the rugged presumptuous face of Kelly Dow.

CHAPTER 13

WEDNESDAY, OCTOBER 3, 12:30 A.M.

Clapp knew Dow, that was plain. He snapped, "How'd you get in here?" as he climbed over the counter to the sidewalk.

Dow had his wallet in one large hairy hand. He opened it pompously and the flash beam glinted on a gold badge. "I showed your roadblock man my deputy sheriff's credentials and he rightly passed me through. I picked up the call on my car radio."

Thursday knew that the homicide chief was yearning for a target on which to vent his rising temper; he listened for the explosion. It didn't come. Instead, Clapp took hold of some leather fringe at Kelly Dow's elbow and walked him away from the booth toward the gleam of Dow's station wagon. A second later, Thursday followed along.

Clapp was saying patiently, ". . . honorary badge doesn't give you any real official status, Mr. Dow. Second place, this is not any business of the sheriff's office."

Dow freed his jacket arm and halted on the sidewalk, facing Clapp. "A thing as serious as this, Lieutenant, I'm surprised to find a solid man like you fiddling with technicalities. Two women have been brutally attacked, *murdered*—and you can't seem to keep the dirty killer in jail!"

"I'm aware of the facts," Clapp said stiffly.

"Facts like that, it's every citizen's duty to do what he can."

"That generally consists of not interfering with police routine. Goodnight, Mr. Dow."

"Routine," said Dow with a snorting laugh. He removed his sun helmet, smoothed back his graying mane with elaborate casualness. "Well, I'm not the kind of slacker who stands by while a madman runs loose through the city choking our women to death. Aren't there any citizens with guts any more?"

"Plenty. Some on the force, believe it or not. Weaver'll get caught."

"Sure he will, sure he will—eventually. But how many helpless women are going to get raped and murdered first?" Dow's hands shook excitedly as he planted his helmet on his head. In a voice like a trumpet, he announced, "That's why I'm calling out my Sunset Riders."

"Mr. Dow," said Clapp between his teeth, "I'm just a policeman; it's not my job to argue about policy. But this is quite different from the Gifford girl case. Then it was just hunting for a kid's body. This time we're tracking down a killer."

"We'll carry rifles, of course," Dow said blandly, his eye shining with grandiose schemes. "All my Riders are honorary deputy sheriffs too. Don't worry about *us* being in danger. Shooting practice every other week."

Thursday butted in harshly, "Did it ever occur to you that Weaver might not be guilty?"

Dow hadn't recognized him before; he peered at Thursday through the gloom. "Say, you here too, Thursday?"

"I asked you a question," Thursday said. "Despite what you or the *Sentinel* or any other half-baked source says, Bliss Weaver still hasn't been convicted of anything. You and your fancy-pants vigilantes shoot him down and you'll be the one sweating out the gas chamber."

"I realize Weaver's your boss but let's not be ridiculous. Since when do you have to convict a mad dog?"

"Ever hear of trial by jury, Dow? A local custom."

"Don't get smart, by thunder. As a citizen I—"

"I see—citizen *you*. Well, Weaver also happens to be a citizen."

Dow bunched up his shoulders angrily and took a half-step forward. He wasn't used to being crossed. "Any time," whispered Thursday, and tightened his hands into fists for the flattening of Kelly Dow. He didn't care if there was an ordinance against doing that to honorary deputy sheriffs or not.

But a new voice called, "Hey, Clapp over there?" and that broke up the fun. "Yeah, here," said Clapp regretfully. His light picked up a slow-moving giant with a placid face, cowlike but for the bitter-cold sea green eyes. The left eye was nearly swollen shut by blue flesh, and the usually peaceable chief of detectives was chewing his gum faster than usual. "What you got, Pensic?"

"What I wanted to ask you," rumbled Pensic in a voice that still showed traces of Middle Europe. "Any Weaver leads down here?"

Clapp shook his head and Kelly Dow seized the chance to win support for his cause. "How's the eye, Lieutenant Pensic? Sorry about your bad luck today—but I was just telling Clapp here we've got to crack down on this thing."

"Who are you?" inquired Pensic, and was told. Then he said, "This case is fouled up with too many outsiders already. Weaver was my baby and he still is. I'll bring him in one way or another."

Thursday liked the rebuff to Dow but he didn't like the anomalous reference to Weaver. "Does that mean with a gun?"

"Another outsider," Pensic said, staring at him. "It means what it says, Thursday. If Weaver plays nice I'll bring him in one way. If he don't, I'll bring him in the other." He shifted his gum. "But I'll bring him in. First prisoner in seventeen years I ever had crush out on me. I don't go for that stuff."

"No, but I don't think you'd care much for killing him either."

Pensic merely laughed shortly, ignored both Thursday and Dow by turning his broad back on them, and said to Clapp, "What are we waiting for?"

"Stein, mainly. The camera crowd too." A uniformed policeman came up and drew Clapp aside. A muttered message, and Clapp swore. "We're not ready for reporters yet! Stall them, keep them happy, sit on them—but don't let them up here."

The cop trotted back the way he'd come. Kelly Dow straightened his fringed jacket, tilted his sun helmet at a confident angle. "Think I'll mosey on. Keep in mind what I said, Lieutenant." And he left them with long strides.

Clapp, watching his direction of departure, swore again. "Ten to one, he's gone to see the newspaper boys, spread his armed posse idea all over the front page."

"Why the kid gloves?" wondered Thursday. "I'd have cracked down so hard he—"

"That's fine for you, citizen. Me, I'm just a lousy civic

employee. Dow's got influence around town. The Chief'll be in a spot, trying to keep Dow bottled up without coming right out and offending the old coot."

"The Chief gets paid for it," growled Pensic. "And maybe some good could be gotten out of this Dow character. He's right—we don't have enough men to guard every unprotected female from here to Mission Valley. He might as well look for Weaver too."

"Well, won't that make us look fine!" Clapp said. "They're still rubbing the Gifford girl in the Chief's face. We merely jailed the killer but Dow stumbled over the body—and right into the headlines. You think he wouldn't be happy to show us up again, take another crack at the city administration. He's been sore ever since his campaign, spent more money than's ever been spent in any campaign here and still didn't get elected mayor."

Thursday said, "What bothers me is what's going to happen to Weaver with a bunch of trigger-happy—"

"Doesn't bother me at all," Pensic interrupted. He looked at the luminous dial of his wristwatch. "Well, maybe you got to stand by the body, Clapp, but I don't. I got a hunt going. See you."

He plodded off into the darkness. Clapp sighed; his anger seemed to have drifted away with Pensic. "Max, I wouldn't be in Weaver's shoes for a million dollars. Mob hysterics like Dow on one side, and cops like Pensic on the other. That's a tough combination to beat."

"Hasn't Dow got anything to do except play cop?"

"He's more or less retired from the drive-in restaurant business. He quit work too young, you know the type, still too much energy not to have a job. Played soldier for a while—that's when his Sunset Riders got started; during the war, an upper-crust civil defense outfit—and then he played politician. But the war's over and his campaign flopped. So now he plays cop. Lucky us."

"Lot of that was talk. Pensic, too."

Headlights swept across the two men. "Over here!" Clapp yelled, waving his arms. The ambulance pulled into the curb. "Where you been?" And then to Thursday, "Weaver should have picked somebody else to slug. Pensic's hard to stir up but Weaver's done it. In a showdown now, all Weaver has to do is look cross-eyed and he'll end up like a Swiss cheese. Pensic's got a national pistol rating."

"He's no killer, even riled."

"No cop is, normally. But there's a guy broke jail, a guy who's killed a couple of women, he's running loose—well, most of the boys have wives and some have daughters. Pensic has both. He's probably put certain ideas over to his men, whether he intended to or not." More spotlights were turned into the sheet-metal booth and Thursday could see Doc Stein's wiry figure bent over the wooden cooler. Clapp said, "Work to do. Better get back to Osborn. She's probably getting lonesome."

But Thursday lingered on the curb after Clapp had left him. He watched the shadows at their grim work under the iron roof; he thought; and presently he walked slowly across the street. But he didn't go toward the police sedan where Merle waited. She might be lonesome, as Clapp had said. But she wasn't as lonesome as Bliss Weaver.

He began to walk faster, heading uptown.

CHAPTER 14

WEDNESDAY, OCTOBER 3, 1:00 A.M.

The alley was pitch black. No light betrayed any life within the House of Buena as Thursday quietly climbed the fire escape up the rear of the shop. He rapped gently at the screen door to the covered porch but there was no response. The screen door wasn't fastened; he groped around inside the porch until he felt an interior door and rapped more peremptorily. Finally he heard Buena Echavez' voice ask his identity and he told her. A circuit breaker buzzed and then he could push open the door into lamplight.

He was in her bedroom once more. She was sitting up in bed against piled pillows. "I was half-expecting you, Mr. Thursday."

"Nonsense." He closed the door behind him and inspected the tapestries that beforehand had been pulled aside on runners to let the door open inward. He commented, "Now that's kind of theatrical, young lady."

"No, you're the theatrical one. The hangings simply hide an unused door." As her bedclothes hid her unused legs. The setting was ideal for her. The bedlamp on her far side limned the fineness of her aristocratic face, cast a nimbus like a crown around her black hair. When she raised her bare arms to make certain her bun was in order, the soft glow revealed the beguiling trace of fuzz on her golden flesh; a golden tone, as usual, muted greenly by the living plants that stood everywhere in the shadows. Her nightgown of heavy white silk was visible from shoulder straps to hips, like a cascade of cream over her voluptuous torso. As if to complete her role of Elizabeth Barrett, a slim volume lay open in her lap. But the book's title was *Mathematical Reformulation of the General Theory of International Trade*.

"Insomnia?" Thursday asked good-naturedly. "Or a guilty conscience?"

She leaned back her head and smiled sleepily at him, her eyes not so frosty tonight. "Why should I feel guilty? Unless some unromantic soul saw you climbing my balcony."

"I mean the laws you break every day. Mind if I sit down?" She let him perch at the foot of her bed. "After all, Buena, you're a criminal."

80

"I told you I can't be touched."

"I discovered you were right. Nothing can be proved. The bets are placed with you face to face so you don't need a flock of telephones. They're paid off at leisure so you don't need a wire service. You have a high-class skittish clientele, social matrons who'd die before they'd confess to the boorish police that they were breaking any laws."

"You have a pretty good mind."

"Average. The key to the whole system is your *above*-average mind. You floored your professors at college, you recognized me this afternoon from the last time I was spread all over the front pages, say, five years ago. Quite a memory, Buena. No betting slips, no records of any kind. You run this whole handbook operation by memory."

She touched her hair again, smiling. "You know all my secrets."

"Nope," he admitted, watching her steadily. "I don't know where your bankroll came from two years ago."

"I came into a little money."

"You were staked to a lot of money. By whom? Coincidence, Joyce Shafto came to town two years ago."

"That won't do," Buena said sharply.

"It's pretty thin, all right. Besides, Joyce is dead and your bankroll paid you a call tonight. That's why your drapes are pulled aside and the porch screen is unlatched. No, nothing on record but you do require that one outside contact, the bankroll. Either it's been here already or you're still waiting up for the visit." He grinned crookedly. "I wonder who it is? Maybe if I spend the night I'll find out."

Though her smile had vanished, the prospect didn't seem to frighten her. She did abruptly pull up her shoulder straps so the peeking tops of her breasts no longer demanded his attention. "Be less crude," she suggested. "Please stop trying to connect me with the death of a redheaded woman twenty miles away."

"But I'm not," he said, and she sat up straight with surprise. "Forgive my crude bluntness, but it's my opinion you had nothing to do with Joyce's murder. It's also my opinion that neither did her husband." He glanced around the room as if Bliss Weaver might pop out of hiding. "But that's just my opinion—unless I can prove it mighty fast, Weaver's likely to get himself killed resisting arrest. You can help me."

"You don't say 'please' very often."

"I do when I'm making a request. I'm *telling* you."

She folded her arms, hugging back her anger. She glared at him arrogantly. "You're barely likeable without the threats Mr. Thursday. With them—ugh! Why don't you believe me when I say I'm not afraid of you?"

"My charm isn't the point at stake. I've been looking for a vise to crack you in, young lady. You beat me with logic. But I'm going to break you without logic—unless you help. Let me show you: there was a second strangling tonight, just a few blocks south of here. The new victim wasn't anybody socially prominent like Joyce, just a poor Mexican girl, identity unknown. The way things stand, Weaver's clipped for that killing also—unless I can offer a substitute." Thursday sized up the woman judiciously. "To start with, you're Mexican too—"

"I'm American!" flared Buena. "Longer than your family, I'll bet."

"Of Mexican descent is a close enough connection. And then there's a tie-up between you and Joyce Shafto, the first victim. Surely somebody will come forward to testify that she got her hair done here. Oh, I can dream up a story that'll curl hair, all right. Have you noticed the *Sentinel*, how they're handling this business in their usual sensitive fashion? They'll go for copy like you, never mind the logic involved." He watched her dark eyes widen, then narrow again. He nodded cheerfully. "You're getting it. I see you're going to help me, Buena."

"But it's ridiculous," she protested faintly. "Ridiculous lies, who'd believe—"

"The *Sentinel* would rather be read than believed. I've got enough news value to get a red-hot theory into print. The sinister House of Buena—how many of your classy clients will be coming in here with their bets after you make the headlines?" He rose to go, saying pleasantly, "Goodnight, then. I can see you're still not afraid of me. Sorry."

"Sit down," she snapped, then added softly, "please." He obeyed. Her soft flesh hid steel, spring steel that was able to bend when necessary. She was giving way now, coolly thoughtful. "I am glad you don't really believe I'm a murderess, Mr. Thursday. You're dreadful enough, as it is."

"Well, stock in trade," Thursday said. "Please don't think I get any bang out of bullying a—" He stopped there.

"A woman," she said, smiling broadly. "We'll pretend you're too kind to call me a cripple. I understand. And I realize what a dear friend this Mr. Weaver must have been to you—" She couldn't comprehend his frown. "Well, what help can I give you?"

"I want to know who the Mexican girl was, what she did, where she came from. If I can get one killing off Weaver's neck, I can probably clear him of both. Your Mexican blood ought to give you contacts on both sides of the border. Your racket ought to give you contacts in other rackets. Somebody, crooked or Mexican, knows who that dead girl is."

"If you'll help me first, out of this bed . . . " She threw back the blanket. Explaining quickly what he knew of the Mexican girl's death and appearance, he hoisted her, one arm around the half-bare smoothness of her back, the other under her gowned helpless legs. Her scented hair tickled his cheek during their brief intimate contact and as he put her down in the wheelchair he was disturbingly conscious of the cleft between her strong breasts.

"You blush," said Buena, amused. "For the record, I don't usually dress with gentlemen present." She inclined her head toward the adjoining office.

Thursday left her alone, keeping the connecting door ajar.

He turned on the overhead light in her matter-of-fact office and listened to Buena wheel around the bedroom, heard the clink of her braces as she adjusted them on her legs. He spotted a small barrel safe in one corner. Quietly, he tried the handle, found it unlocked. Nothing was kept in it but several neat bundles of currency.

"Exactly two thousand three hundred and fifteen dollars," Buena called to him from the next room. Guiltily, Thursday closed the safe door. As if she had seen him, Buena laughed. "I never lock my safe. Wouldn't want it smashed open by burglars."

"Well, there's logic," he said. When she called him back into the bedroom, he found that she had donned a white silk peignoir to match her nightgown. At the shoulder she had pinned another of the red camellias such as had adorned her hair that afternoon.

He said, "You and flowers seem to get along pretty well."

"Not cut ones," she said. She wrinkled her nose at her jungle of potted plants. "But this having one's outdoors indoors sometimes makes for dirt on the floor." Without a break in voice or change in expression, she commenced speaking in Spanish, a torrent of words. Thursday couldn't follow beyond the opening phrase, which was, "My dear pumpkinhead, at this late hour . . ." Buena, satisfied with the result of her experiment, wheeled herself into the office and shut the door firmly.

Thursday lingered by the closed door, listening to the click of the telephone dial, her indistinct voice. Though he could hear little and understand less, it seemed to him that Buena's Spanish was more the formalized lisping Castilian taught in public schools than the smoother Mexican dialect. He smoked a cigar, then another, wondering if she was up to some trick and not knowing what to do about it anyway. Discovering a dart board on the wall, a bull's-eye target of bright circles, he played at tossing the feathered spikes. His low scores disgusted him and he laid the darts aside on the bedstand and decided he'd better stick to handball. He began to perspire, trusting Buena less and less, and he lit a third cigar, his flame shaky.

It was past three o'clock in the morning when Buena rolled out of her office, looking hot but rather pleased. She said, "We'll have a visitor shortly. Under a flag of truce, as it were. What's the term—a man who shall be nameless?"

"Okay, fine. No tricks, though."

"Why, certainly not." She laughed softly. "Now we're both afraid. Do you think some hot chocolate would settle our nerves? It's surprisingly cooling." She made a pot of the thick Mexican drink in her kitchenette across the hall. He watched her from the doorway, then they drank it in the bedroom and chatted pleasantly, recalling State College which they had attended at quite different times and with far different scholarship.

It was nearly four o'clock when the chime sounded downstairs, Thursday rose, tense and on guard, but Buena said, "I'll see to it." She went alone to admit the visitor, piloting her chair skillfully down the ramp. Thursday waited, listened to the mumble of voices below. Then she was returning, a man pushing her up the incline. They all met at the edge of the mezzanine, in the half-light.

"Mr. Thursday," said Buena politely, "meet Mr. Nameless."

CHAPTER 15

WEDNESDAY, OCTOBER 3, 4:00 A.M.

Thursday said nothing and they continued into the bedroom. Buena parked by the head of her bed, tilting the lampshade so that Mr. Nameless could be studied more easily. Thursday eyed him coldly, letting the silence sink in. Nameless shuffled his feet, suddenly and tardily took off his shapeless blue felt hat, and scratched his shaggy butch haircut. "Cheap operator" was written all over his squat figure: in the flashy cut of his coffee-brown suit with its brass key chain dangling, in the sullen reddish eyes, in the predatory mouth. Although his apish face was oily with apprehension, he met Thursday's scrutiny with an obsequious boldness learned in the brighter lights of many a police showup.

Finally, in a whisky croak, he dared, "Well, is this about something or not?"

From the shadows, Buena said, "I haven't talked to him, Mr. Thursday. I've never seen him before. I simply used my, ah, contacts as you suggested."

"Just doing a friend a favor," Nameless said uneasily. Thursday understood. Under his callous surface, Nameless was mushy with fear; someone had put an "or else" ultimatum to him. "Make it quick and easy, hey guy? Big deal up north. I was on my way out of town—"

"I'd be too if I'd just killed a girl."

Nameless gave a frightened whinny. "Now I didn't have nothing to do with *that!*"

"You know who did."

"What's this cop talk? Wait up now, what kind of shake you giving me?" He would have been out the door but Thursday was already blocking the way.

"You haven't been crossed, not yet," Thursday said harshly. "But the way it goes is up to you." He reached out and flipped Nameless's earlobe.

Nameless backed up a step, rubbing his ear. "Don't have to get personal like that. I don't want to mix it with nobody. I was promised—they said nothing'd happen if I come, that's why I come—"

"Tell me about the girl and nothing will. What do you know about her?"

"Nothing," was the instinctive response. Then he saw Thursday's expression and backed farther out of reach. "I mean nothing especial."

86

"Name?"

"Ana Maria—Ana Maria Zagal—from around Tijuana same as the rest of my girls. Understand, guy, I didn't know her. She come to me and if they're big enough they're old enough so I brought her up here yesterday with the rest of them."

"What for?"

"Hey guy, ladies present." Nameless shot a flustered glance at Buena, motionless in her wheelchair. "Well, I rent this old house off Market—*you* know. Once in a while I bring up a load of gals from T-town for a day or two. Everybody happy, no harm done."

Thursday regarded him with steely disgust. Nameless was a pimp; the dead girl had been one of his hustlers. Despite being a border town, a sailor and tourist town, San Diego had long been free of organized prostitution. Lieutenant Richards and his vice squad had seen to that. But a fly-by-night house, staffed by Tijuana chippies, operating at the longest for three nights in a row—that would be almost impossible to locate and raid. Only Thursday's desire for information overcame his urge to kick Nameless all the way down the ramp. "Then why'd you kill her? Wouldn't she kick in?"

"Stop aiming at me—I didn't do it! It was the big guy, him."

Thursday's breath caught. Nameless had actually seen the strangler! "What big guy? What's his name?"

"I don't know, just a guy. We don't ask names. Ana Maria brought him in around ten p.m. I just saw his back, going down the hall. A big blond guy."

It struck Thursday almost as a physical blow. The fugitive Bliss Weaver was certainly big and his sandy hair could easily be described as blond. By no stretch of the imagination could that description be tailored to fit Scarmouth, thin and little. "Come on, come on, what else did he look like?"

"Well, beats me, guy. We keep it plenty dim, makes it homier." With a crook's sure instinct, Nameless realized the pressure was off. "One of the other broads was moaning about it, saying Ana Maria sure drew a handsome one."

A handsome one. Again the finger pointed directly at Weaver.

He took it out on Nameless, who was beginning to smile condescendingly. "So you stood around counting your money while he strangled the poor kid."

"Now that ain't the way!" Nameless protested, whining. Thursday listened to the rest of the sordid story. How, after time had gone by, Nameless thought to check up on Ana Maria Zagal. How he had found her choked to death and the big blond man gone out the back way. How the other girls had scattered instantly, leaving Nameless alone with a naked corpse. He blanched at the memory. "Well, *I* wasn't going to take the fall, that's for sure. I got her clothes onto her and hauled her in my car over to that ranch market—it's only a couple blocks away, understand—and ditched her, figuring what's done is done and nobody's ever—"

"What about her shoes?"

"Couldn't get them on her feet, they was that swelled up. I just stuck them in the car and tossed them out someplace later."

"You keep her purse too?"

"The big guy must've took it. I'm screwed if I know why—it was clean."

"Clean, why? Ana Maria just work for the fun of it?"

"They collected beforehand and I always collected from them right after, tips and all." Nameless winked, full of ancient wisdom. "Then I always give the gals their cut when I take them back across the border, minus a little for round-trip fare, of course. I couldn't have them maybe deciding to run out with the whole take, hey? You know women."

"I thought I did," whispered Buena suddenly from her dark retreat. "But now I'm not so sure. Why any woman, no matter how low, would have anything to do with a slimy—" Her voice rose and broke with anger.

Nameless drew himself up. "Now let's remember I don't have to hang around here and take any—"

"Oh, don't you?" asked Buena softly as her wheelchair rolled forward sparkling into the lamplight. The pistol in her hand pointed at the pimp's face.

Nameless gave another whinny of fright and shrank sideways against a tall rubber plant. The glossy leaves shook with his trembling. Thursday stood where he was, eyeing the gun, a practical little .25 revolver. Nameless whimpered hoarsely, "Hey, you give me your word!"

"It only counts between human beings." Buena was flushed, eyes shining, breath coming quick with excitement. "Mr. Thursday, he's your prisoner. Call the police."

Thursday spoke to Nameless instead. "Get out of here."

Nameless huddled against the rubber plant, gaping at the gun. *"She's going to shoot at me!"*

"She's not going to do anything." As Buena stared in astonishment, he walked across the room and took the pistol from her hand. He replaced it in the bedstand and closed the drawer. "You were leaving town. Make sure you do. And make double sure you never come back."

"Sure, you bet. You know I won't." Nameless sidled for the door. "Glad to be of service. No offense, hey? Okay?" His back filled the doorway.

A strangled sound in her throat, Buena reached behind her on the bedstand. Then her hand flung out viciously at his departing figure and the feathers of a toy dart appeared magically sticking out of his shoulder. Nameless stopped short, glanced back at her apologetically. "No offense," he mumbled. He reached behind and plucked the steel-spiked dart loose from his shoulder and dropped it on the floor. "No offense." And they heard him scuttle down the ramp, and the bang of the street door.

Thursday picked up the dart and punched it carefully into the bull's-eye of the wall target. "Been a shame to break up the set."

"I don't care! I only wish I'd—" Buena bit her lip while her rage subsided. Finally she said, "I'll never be able to understand you at all."

"The last thing I want is for the cops to get that description out of him. I'm trying to get Weaver out of the gas chamber, not put him in deeper."

"But that obscene little animal—he deserves . . ."

Thursday shook his head tiredly. "Who am I to say what anybody deserves?"

"What you mean is," said Buena, flushing deeper, "who am *I* to say?"

"I meant what I said, that's all. Nothing between the lines. I'm not subtle." He glanced at his watch; night was nearly over. "I've got to shove off. Thanks for everything."

"Will you lift me back into bed, please?" He did, and this time her body was rigid against him. She pulled the blanket over her braces and opened the peignoir to slip it off. She looked up at him from the pillows and asked quietly, "Why don't I despise you?"

"Don't you?"

"No." She shrugged and the heavy silk of the nightgown dipped open in front. She looked down at herself, still breathing heavily from high emotion. "It's a lonely life at this time of morning, everything gone but one's desires. Are you lonely often?"

"Often."

She seized his wrist. "Touch me," she commanded. She guided his hand onto the warm smooth slopes of her breasts.

"It's the time of morning," he murmured, and gently tried to extricate his hand. She closed her eyes and stubbornly forced it deeper. They stayed that way a moment, very still, and then she sighed and smiled and opened her eyes. He withdrew his hand.

"Perhaps someday you'll find time for a purely social call," she said in her normal voice. She unpinned the velvet-red camellia from her robe. "Just to remind you. This kind is called a Princess Bacciochi." She fastened the blossom in his lapel as a boutonniere.

He looked down at it, embarrassed, but glad to escape her moist eyes. "Thanks, Buena. It's a pretty kind, all right."

"Red's my favorite." Something cruel lurked behind her eyes

as she added cryptically, "Red was the color of Judas' hair."

He didn't understand the reference, the last-minute change in her. He grinned, said goodnight louder than he intended and backed away. Her own goodnight was the merest whisper but Thursday fancied he could still hear it as he stood again at the top of the fire escape in the alley blackness. He hesitated before descending the steel stairway, wondering. He could see nothing below. The flower worried him. He didn't know to whom Buena had spoken on the telephone; perhaps the red blossom was meant to finger him.

He murmured aloud the name Judas. He jerked the flower loose and dropped it at his feet. But then he remembered Bliss Weaver, somewhere else in the night. Thursday knelt and began striking matches to discover where the camellia lay. Because if the red petals were supposed to mark him for an attack, why then perhaps the attack might provide an answer of sorts.

He found the camellia again, replaced it in his buttonhole. He got to his feet thoughtfully. The match flare had revealed more than a discarded flower. In the wavering light, he had seen a small heap of recent tobacco ash, pipe dottle that had been knocked out at the top of the fire escape. Buena had received another backstairs visitor that night.

CHAPTER 16

WEDNESDAY, OCTOBER 3, 5:00 A.M.

Austin Clapp had his feet up on the desk, his eyes nearly closed, his ear cocked to the drone of the radio. He grunted irritably at Thursday's entrance. Thursday scraped up a chair, sat down and, uninvited, read the autopsy report on Joyce

Shafto. The chair felt good after walking twenty blocks crosstown from the House of Buena to police headquarters. The autopsy form might as well have stayed blank; the tamales in the dead woman's stomach didn't help specify time of death because no one knew when she'd eaten them.

Between routine disturbances and check-in calls, the radio voice made frequent impersonal mentions of XP-1. That would be top code for Bliss Weaver—Escaped Prisoner One.

Clapp opened his eyes. "We've pulled back all men on leave, canceled all time off till we get him. Roadblocks on the highways, depot inspections, and the immigration boys are watching the border. Kind of ridiculous, actually—us slaving to stop Weaver from leaving town when we'd just as soon he was somewhere else."

"Usual phony leads?"

"Not yet, not until the morning papers. Then we'll have him spotted everywhere from here to Yuma. Course, in the meantime, Dow and his riders of the purple sage are making up for it."

"I wondered about that."

"Yeah, they're in our hair already. Big call to arms, all the society vigilantes are saddled and bridled and armed to the teeth. They've been poking into every canyon and under every tumbleweed in town." Clapp laughed viciously. "One of them fell off his horse and broke his arm. Too bad it wasn't Dow."

"Give him time."

"We're not giving him much. First complaint we get—discharged gun, trespassing, anything—we clamp down on Dow's bunch as a public menace. That's orders from up top."

A knock on the door, and a uniformed cop came in with a stack of newspapers, sunrise editions. He left them on the desk and went away again, yawning. Clapp made no move to touch them so Thursday picked up the top one, the *Sentinel*. SECOND MURDER SPURS HUNT FOR MAD STRANGLER. . . . Thursday winced. He said, "Where's Merle?"

"Catching some shuteye down in the matron's office.

Which suits me fine." Clapp grimaced. "We've got a stake-out on her apartment and a tap on her phone, in case Weaver tries to reach her. So long as Osborn hangs around here we don't have to assign a man to her. A man I couldn't spare anyway." He gazed curiously across the desk. "What smells so bad?"

"Read this." Frowning, Thursday pushed the front page toward Clapp, his finger impaling the two-column boldface box under the headlines. The message was simple and dramatically terse: in the interest of public safety, the *Sentinel* would pay one thousand dollars reward for any information leading to the capture—dead or alive—of Bliss Weaver.

Clapp read it without interest. "So what?"

"Ask Merle 'so what.' The *Sentinel's* never had that kind of money. Who put it up? And why—why this constant picking on Weaver? Every time I turn around—"

"You've got a bad conscience. The *Sentinel's* got a heartful of civic interest. Says so right here. But just to be doing something . . . " Clapp cradled the phone against his shoulder, began drumming with his yellow pencil. After a few minutes' waiting, he reached the man he sought, the *Sentinel's* managing editor. Followed another few minutes of casual conversation before Clapp edged in with the question he'd called about. Thursday fidgeted while Clapp listened blandly, grunting "uh-huh" and "no kidding?" now and then.

Finally Clapp muffled the phone with a big hand and said, "The money source is confidential. He's been pumping me full of bellywash about the ethics of journalism—sounds like a private cop. I think he's fishing, wants to trade me a scoop for a scoop."

"Hold him," said Thursday. He picked the pencil out of Clapp's fist and scribbled quickly along the top margin of the newspaper. "Sell him that." He had written: *Second strangle victim—Ana Maria Zagal, Tijuana.*

Clapp's feet hit the floor with a crash. He glared across the desk. "Max, if this is a gag—"

"No gag. Sell it to him. You can't get hurt."

Finally, Clapp put the receiver to his head again, his eyes

never leaving Thursday's face as he bartered with the *Sentinel* editor, trading one name for another—but being careful to label his information as "unverified" and "from a strictly unofficial source." At last he hung up.

"Well?" said Thursday.

"Now I think you better talk," said Clapp, leaning back. "You trade me, and it better be good."

They locked gazes and Thursday gave way and told his story. He knew Clapp was perfectly capable of locking him up for obstructing justice if he didn't talk. And, thinking of Merle and her woes, he had no desire to be put out of commission at this stage of the game.

So he told about Nameless the pimp. He left out Nameless' description of the murderer, since he had no desire to reinforce the case against Weaver. Nor did he mention Buena Echavez because he'd made a pact with her, although he suspected she had several other motives for helping him, possibly stronger ones than the fear-motive she had succumbed to.

Which left him with a first hand description and the second hand testimony of an unknown procurer.

"Well, that's not much," said Clapp suspiciously, resurveying the notes he'd taken. "Where off Market Street was this so-and-so's house? Where was he going from here?"

"I don't know," said Thursday. He wasn't in any hurry to have Nameless picked up, for Weaver's sake. "I was lucky to get that much, the identification of the girl, what happened to her shoes, how she got put in that cooler."

Clapp grunted. He picked up the phone again and called the office of the chief of detectives to pass on the tentative identification for further work. Then he rang the autopsy room downstairs for the same purpose. Between calls he muttered to Thursday, "I ought to make you sweat for this, but— the guy who posted the thousand reward for Weaver's hide is Kelly Dow. Wouldn't you know?"

Thursday blinked. "No, I wouldn't know," he said softly. A couple of hitherto unconnected details began to fall into place in his mind, and he tried to account for this new perspective:

the continued unhealthy interest that Dow was taking in the fate of Bliss Weaver. What was the link between the two men?

Dow had taken Weaver's attorney to lunch the day after the first strangling. At that time, possibly, the insanity angle had been bullied out of the easy-going Ivah Hecht. This hypothesis explained how the *Sentinel* had gotten wind of the "mad uncle" story so quickly, how Thursday's own connection with the case had become public knowledge. And, feeding on itself, this view of Dow's actions grew to a single gruesome conclusion: *Dow wanted Weaver dead.*

There it was, reasonless, circumstantial. But Thursday couldn't shake the idea off. For one wild moment he tried to picture Kelly Dow as the strangler of Joyce Shafto and the Mexican girl. Yet he couldn't make the least sense of that.

Dow was turning every available weapon, including public opinion, against Weaver. He had even tipped the newspaper to hinder Thursday's work. Or—his mind did an uncomfortable flipflop—had it been meant to help? For Hecht was also Kelly Dow's attorney, and Hecht might have hired Thursday to work for Dow instead of Weaver. That would account for Hecht's worrisome tightrope act, his insistence on the importance of the dragon compact. It might be Dow to whom possession of Joyce Shafto's compact was a life and death matter.

". . . should be on my knees, giving thanks," growled Clapp, hanging up the phone again. "But I suddenly recall I'm going to be in dutch with the *Union-Tribune* boys. I'll have to think up some big news for them or they'll be yelling favoritism. Oh, thanks, Max."

"Have a heart. You've got the whole city on your team. You're trying to catch a guy you've got taped down to the mole between his toes. I'm trying to find a guy I've never even seen, all by my lonesome. Don't begrudge me one anonymous tip."

"You still punching away at that apartment prowler-purse snatcher routine?" Clapp inquired sarcastically. "The little scarred guy with hands like a gorilla?"

The answer, despite the disconcerting emergence of Kelly

Dow, was yes. But Thursday found himself on shaky ground; he tried to shift his position slightly. "Maybe we should forget about Scarmouth for the time being. Maybe that isn't the baby we're after. Suppose, theoretically, he's a big blond man—"

"Oh," snarled Clapp, "so now the strangler is Bliss Weaver's twin. Just exactly like Weaver except a different person, huh?"

"Now, I didn't say that. Weaver's not exactly blond. And he's not the only big nonbrunet in town."

"You keep up that kind of talk and I'll think he's not the only maniac in town either."

"You keep making fun of me and I won't let you do me any more favors." He grinned at the expression on Clapp's face. "How about checking your m. o. files? You've got modus operandi for every thief in the country. There might be one fits what I'm looking for. Or if you won't, I've got an insurance friend who will and then I might be one up on you."

Clapp drummed with his pencil, finally pursed his lips and rose to his feet. "You'd make a fortune selling vacuum cleaners. You can't be insulted."

Clapp stalked out. Thursday lit a cigar and closed his eyes. Suddenly scared, he thought, What if I'm never able to prove I'm right? What if I'm off on the wrong track and when I find it out, it'll be too late?

And then Clapp was standing just inside the door, a machine-punched file card in his hand. "Say, you sure you didn't make this whole thing up from old Wanted circulars?"

"Don't tell me I called one right!"

"Gasman Casey Lee," Clapp read from the card. "Various aliases. Six-two, two hundred twenty pounds, *white* hair and blue eyes. Was in Leavenworth up to two years ago. His m.o. was to pick on single females in apartments, use that gas spray trick you mentioned to get in, scare the women silly and walk off with their valuables. Present whereabouts unknown."

Thursday came to his feet. "It fits—he's in San Diego!"

Clapp gave him a sweet smile. "This one's on me, pal. I left

96

out a detail. The Gasman was sixty-three years old when he died two years ago in Leavenworth, was buried there. You bet his present whereabouts is unknown." He chuckled soundlessly, sat down again with his feet propped up, and turned the radio's mutter a little higher. "Now why don't you go home and let me catch Weaver my way?"

CHAPTER 17

WEDNESDAY, OCTOBER 3, 6:00 A.M.

Thursday sank into his chair again, suddenly dog-tired as if he had been climbing for hours against a summit still hidden in swirling mists. Vaguely, lost in gray thoughts, he understood Clapp was continuing to rib him. ". . . . single brilliant connection between Casey Lee and Joyce Shafto. Lee was buried in prison because nobody claimed the body. Now if somebody doesn't claim the redhead's body pretty soon, I'll have her stuffed and presented to you by the mayor. Say, where's your sense of humor?"

"Yeah, where's yours?" Thursday asked with a fish-eyed pitying glance. "I'm not beat yet. So Gasman Lee is dead and buried. That doesn't mean his methods are. He was in the pokey, he had cellmates. Maybe the Gasman passed along his modus operandi, his spray gadget idea and all, to a friend. Leavenworth'll know who his friends were."

Clapp looked at the five-dollar bill Thursday had laid on the desk. "Just what do you think that's for?"

"I know you—you won't burden the taxpayers. That's for the long telegram you're going to send Leavenworth."

"Send it yourself."

"They'll answer you faster. Who were Gasman's buddies and what about them."

Clapp began to laugh it off. Then he regarded Thursday gravely. "You've gone off your rocker on this whole thing— you know that, don't you, son? Okay, it's your dough." He thumbed the five into his watchpocket, massaged his ear wryly, then put the receiver to it again. "I'll charge it to my home phone."

He was spelling out names to the girl at the telegraph office when Jim Crane sauntered in, mouth tight and disgusted, a dirty-blue swelling on his forehead. He gingerly removed his panama, landed it on the hat tree and lounged against the wall. Though peeved, the white-haired detective-sergeant seemed fresher than the other two men.

"How's the head?" Thursday asked him.

"Great. But you ought to see that windshield."

Clapp finished the phone call. He told Thursday, "There's five bucks shot," and asked Crane what luck.

"None. I laid off ten blocks on every side of Ranchers Market and searched every gutter, trashcan and vacant lot. No sign of her shoes and purse."

"As it turns out, the shoes don't matter anyway," said Thursday.

"Oh, you're way behind, Jim," Clapp said sarcastically. "Our boy Max has cracked the whole deal. He got a spirit message." Thursday grinned weakly and reeled off the reconstruction of the second murder for Crane who listened closely. The telephone rang into the conversation. Clapp said, "Bet it's Western Union calling back to see if it's a gag or . . ." But it turned out to be business, according to the change in Clapp's voice. "Yeah. Good. When'll she get here? Thanks." Hanging up, he announced, "Pensic has verified identification with the Tijuana police."

Thursday couldn't work up any interest in that. He played halfheartedly with a half-dollar, attempting the trick of making the coin walk across his knuckles.

"Ana Maria Zagal, sixteen years old, on their books as a semi-pro hustler. Tijuana's checked her address on Avenida

Cinco de Mayo, she's not home, her mother doesn't know where she is. Left yesterday morning, supposedly to shop in our town. Clothes she wore match all right, Pensic says. The old lady's catching a bus up now to take the final look. Oh— the missing purse is red straw, medium-sized."

Crane waved his hand to indicate he was thinking. "This Mexican kid comes up here to raise shopping money. Weaver's broke and on the run. Maybe sight of a prowl car scares him into this cathouse, where the Zagal girl starts a fuss. He silences her, takes her purse and lights out again."

"No," said Thursday stubbornly. His coin trick failed again but he kept at it. "The strangler—a person unknown—accompanied the Zagal girl into the house, intending to rob her. Hustlers are supposed to be easy pickings. Goodnight—can you see *Weaver* doing a thing like that?"

"Why, yes," said Crane. "My idea of Weaver is not a kindly one." The half-dollar fumbled out of Thursday's hand and rang loudly on the floor. Crane picked it up, studied it, flipped it back to him. "And the snapper is supposed to be that the purse was empty?"

"The pimp said he took charge of money earned."

"That's the usual, all right. But the girl was a Mexican national, just up from Tijuana. Maybe she had a few centavos with her, maybe even a peso or two." Crane leaned forward, pointing an emphatic forefinger. "Look, we know Weaver is flat broke. What if she did have some Mexican money in that purse and he tries to spend it? Because there's so much American money used in Tijuana, why, Mexican coins are pretty rare on our side of the border . . . "

"It's a long chance, Jim," said Clapp slowly. "But darned if it isn't a move. We could put out a screener for anybody passing Mexican coins. Have the vending companies check their cigarette machines—"

"Weaver smokes a pipe," Thursday objected.

"But Weaver doesn't have a pipe. Maybe the bus drivers have caught something in their boxes, or the pay phones—

something like that could give us a fix on Weaver, the neighborhood where he's gone to earth."

Thursday closed his mouth suddenly and put his half-dollar away. This police reasoning didn't only apply to Weaver; it would work also for the big blond prowl-thief who seemed to be as broke as Weaver. If Weaver was innocent, this particular police net couldn't harm him. Furthermore, Thursday could supplement the coin hunt with his own people, his operatives and his carefully cultivated list of helpful contacts. He smiled bemusedly at Crane who didn't understand why.

". . . Jim, so get it started before you knock off," Clapp was saying. "And tell Bryan or whoever's on that I want a house-by-house search along Market Street, two blocks leeway, south side first, to locate where the Zagal girl was strangled. May be prints or something that'll help us." Startled, he suddenly noticed his notes about Nameless still among the papers on his desk. "Holy smoke, I meant to get this pimp's description on the air."

Both policemen cleared out, leaving Thursday sitting alone. In a few moments he heard his own words come back to him through the loudspeaker, and he sighed. Aware of the lethargy creeping up on him, he roused himself from the chair and wandered out into the corridor. Down the way, he saw the dark door lettered MATRON. He hesitated, picturing Merle asleep, escaped for the moment beyond reality. Then he walked down the echoing corridor and opened the door quietly.

She was huddled on the folding cot in the corner of the unlit office, fully dressed, striped with the first dawnlight through the barred window. Sleep hadn't meant escape for her; as Thursday stood over her, she twisted and whimpered like a child. Thursday knelt down and slid his arm under her shoulders. "Merle," he whispered. "Merle, better wake up, honey."

She shuddered violently and then relaxed against his arm. The familiar warm pressure recalled the tender sense of belonging and immediately Thursday felt the cold thrust of guilt. He was a stranger now. And when she mumbled, "Oh,

Bliss . . . most terrible dream . . . " he withdrew his arm and stood up again.

Her eyes blinked open and she stared up at him, frightened. "Max—oh, you're here! Has anything happened?"

"Nothing new," he said brusquely. He was glad she hadn't caught him in his instant of softness, yet at the same time he despised that second-best sort of gladness. "Are you awake yet? We've got work to do."

"I think so." She sat up clumsily, straightened her clothes. "All right, what is it? What *can* be done, Max?"

He told her about the Mexican coin possibility and made her repeat it to be certain she understood. "You've got contacts, plenty of them, left over from your job. Start calling them, get them asking around. That's what I'm going to do with my bunch."

"A big man? A blond man?" she asked in a thin voice.

"It's definitely not Weaver," he assured her for the third time. "Come on—let's get to it. You and I and the cops will have this town covered. Just think, one beat-up Mexican dime might turn the trick."

She looked through him. Her tousled head drooped. "Thanks for trying, Max." She made no move to rise.

"What kind of talk is that?"

"We *would* have been happy together, I mean Bliss and I. You didn't know him, nobody knows him. He was tired of the ratrace he'd had up to then, he wanted to have kids, a big home. He was tired of everything he knew, except me. I know sometimes he blustered to other people, but he was never, never anything but gentle with me. But what changed? What blew everything skyhigh?"

He grabbed the front of her dress and yanked her to her feet. Through the material he could feel her breasts breathe high with anger. "I'm ashamed of you," he rasped into her face. "Ashamed I ever loved a weak sister like you."

Eyes blazing wide, she said, "Get away with your dirty hands," and stomped her heel down on his instep.

He let loose and backed away a step, managing to grin.

"That's better, that's the old adrenalin. Now cut the palaver and get on the phone. Never forget—*Weaver's not guilty*."

But as he turned to go, he heard Merle's hopeless whisper behind him. "Are you sure?"

Clapp was standing in the open doorway and Thursday said, "Don't miss anything," brushing by. He walked down the corridor, trying to limp as little as possible. He could hear her begin spinning the telephone dial.

Clapp caught his arm at the corridor's end where dawn was turning the overhead bulbs sickly. Clapp said softly, "You hate this Weaver's guts. Yet you're tearing yourself apart to save him."

"I thought you said I was off my rocker."

"You're trying to save him so Osborn can have him instead of you?"

"I'm just trying to save him."

"That adds up to the same thing."

"I never was good at arithmetic, Clapp, not when it was people." He shrugged irritably. "You said I couldn't ever make up for that handkerchief stunt. It's even worse now I know I tried to frame an innocent man. Well, maybe you've been right all along. But all I can do is bust a gut trying."

"I didn't mean you should take it this hard," Clapp murmured. "Get some sleep. Don't play martyr *and* sucker, not with it a thousand to one against you."

Through the tan stucco archway was the morning, the earliest cars being disgorged from the Coronado ferry, a massive mechanical street sweeper clanking back to its cave, a switch engine leisurely pulling along a string of fat freight cars in the half-awake light.

A new day, its air smelling of the age-old fragile hope that this was an important day. In the miles around were a half million people about to get up and find out. The street lamps graciously died in unison as far as the two men could see.

"I'll give you better odds than that," said Thursday. "Out of a half million population, I'm the only sucker who honestly thinks Bliss Weaver isn't a murderer."

CHAPTER 18

Sleep was burning at his eyelids by the time he'd driven home to his half of the duplex. Sleep and something worse, as he stared dejectedly around a living room that had never before looked so dingy, his tired brain heavy with the realization that Merle's loving presence would never again brighten this lonely place.

Not if he won. And if he lost, he'd never dare meet her eyes or look closely at himself.

He dragged into the kitchen and sat down at the table and placed the telephone before him, after brushing a few crumbs out of the way. He patiently made call after call, his operatives first, then his contacts.

"Hal? Thursday. Got a job for you."

"Better be good, this time of morning."

"It's important, spend what you have to. Look for a guy. Name unknown, but here's the description: big fellow, blond or blondish, good-looking, must be the open-faced type since having women trust him is his racket. May have overalls and tool kit in his possession. Not much else to go on except he's so broke he may be passing Mexican pesos or smaller Mexican coins—"

"Slow down. You talking about this crazy Weaver guy?"

"I said I didn't know his name, didn't I? If you should run across Weaver or any sign of him, ring me right away. Don't follow it up or try to start anything, just call me so I can shepherd him safe into headquarters. Don't worry about Weaver, anyway. It's this other big boy I want a line on. Oh, and while you're at it, watch for a little fellow with a scarred mouth . . ."

As some white magic abruptly cleared his brain, he came near to dropping the receiver. Of course! His teeth chattered over this new obvious idea that had taken so long to break through. He wasn't looking for one man, he was looking for *two*—a *team* of prowlers! Scarmouth would be the brains, the chief, the one who cased the robberies. But he was too sinister in appearance to make the entrances; no lone woman would open the door for him, gas spray or no gas spray. So the blond handsome one, Big Boy, was the front for the final operation of getting inside the apartment. That and only that would knit up the disturbing holes in his theory.

"Hey, Thursday—your arteries harden or something?"

"Got hit by lightning. Is everything straight now? Look for a big blond guy and a little thin scarmouth guy, probably bumming around together. Don't bother with the big hotels or high-class areas—these boys are prowlers who haven't made a haul lately, broke and hiding out. And don't forget the Mexican coin angle. You start with the waterfront and . . . "

He assigned districts to his other three operatives and then went down his long list of friendly tipsters—smoke shop operators, bartenders, hotel and depot detectives. He called the business manager of a string of supermarkets: one of his personnel checking clients. He alerted the assistant circulation boss of the *Sentinel* (a close-mouthed trustworthy fellow he'd met through Merle) to have his paper carriers watch for Big Boy and Scarmouth. The head of the Navy's shore patrol detail was a friend from Thursday's service days; he promised to pass the word along. And so on.

When he finally replaced the receiver his left hand was wet and stiff from having clutched it so long. But he felt good, active; he had accomplished something, casting out a dragnet of considerable size. Furthermore his mind was eager with his new tack, the angle that there were two men involved, not just one with irreconcilable characteristics. He left the kitchen and flopped on his flowered divan, ready for some serious thinking.

It was only by awakening convulsively, bathed in sweat, that he knew he had been asleep. His wristwatch said two in the afternoon and the tight-closed, blinds-drawn little living room was like an oven. He shook his head groggily and stumbled outdoors into the torrid sunshine, furious with himself for wasting five precious hours, for being too knuckleheaded to set the alarm clock. The world might have ended while he slept like a fool.

Without shaving, without changing, still wearing the wilted red camellia as a signal on his lapel, he climbed into his sedan and ran it downtown.

As he climbed out onto the yellow dirt of the police parking lot, he got a booming shout, "Not many vags turn in here voluntarily!" Thursday blinked around and saw the fierce godless grin of John D. Meier. He was a short heavy-set powerhouse, black-haired and bushy browed, believing in nothing. He was the local insurance claims investigator for a score of companies. Today, in his suit of gray-and-white seersucker, he looked as cool and neat as a marble headstone.

"This is a disguise," Thursday said. "Dodging insurance agents."

"Who'd underwrite a risk like you? Buy you coffee." As Thursday hesitated, "You might as well. If you're in on the Weaver case—that's what I read—Clapp's out eating. I just found out myself."

"Sold." They fell in step across the parking lot, heading toward the short order counter on the opposite corner. "Anything broken on Weaver?"

"Oh sure, developments are promised soon. I have the word of the desk sergeant for it." Meier grinned cynically, bowed Thursday through the screen door of the cafe. They slid into a booth and ordered coffee.

"What's your angle?" asked Thursday. "Was Weaver into your companies for something?"

"Nope, but his dear departed wife was. Rock insurance. Shafto had her jewelry insured to the hilt and I've been keeping an eye peeled for some time. Ever meet her? I made it a point to, didn't trust her. Most of her junk was sold or pawned in the six months since the separation, as you probably know."

"It's legal."

"Okay, but go back *nine* months. She put in a theft claim on her big item, a bracelet, six square-cut emeralds in a lace-silver mount." Thursday remembered all too easily; it was while covering the theft story that Merle had first become acquainted with Bliss Weaver. "Shafto claimed it was stolen in a purse she left lying around on a nightclub table. Had worn the stones to a cocktail party but took them off in later evening. Careless, but that's an idiot for you, and she was within the limitations. We put out the usual lines and offers but didn't get a nibble; the bracelet has never turned up." The coffee came and Meier tried it. Too hot. "Of course, I was born doubting my mother."

Thursday said, slowly stirring his coffee, "Then you think Joyce faked the theft."

"I always begin with that assumption. Nothing's happened to prove me wrong. That's why I've been checking her inventory for the bracelet, thinking she might have hidden it and claimed it was stolen to get cash. You know, have her cake and eat it too." He spread his hands. "But no catchem. Maybe I misjudged the poor wench. Though burn me if I can figure how the emeralds were fenced without my hearing about it eventually."

"Yes," said Thursday and then was silent for a while, Meier's shrewd eyes watching him. Meier could sense there was more in the air than grease from the fry kitchen. He prompted with, "We've done good business before, Max. Let me in if you've got anything."

"Thinking, I don't know, maybe. I'm working for Weaver. I claim he isn't guilty. Now you bring this jewel thing up and—let's just suppose your suspicions have been right, as usual. That Joyce Shafto's bracelet was never stolen, that she's been keeping it cached in her apartment."

"Keep interesting me."

"Let's say she got it out to parade around in, the night she happened to be strangled. She was human, she'd get it out occasionally to play with in private. Emeralds would go perfect with that slinky green dress she died in. Now the strangler eased in there to rob her—that's my theory, not Clapp's—but when she died on him, he got rattled. He stopped searching for valuables, snatched the bracelet and beat it. There's a scratch on Joyce's arm, inside forearm near the elbow, that's never been explained. Clapp thinks it happened in the struggle. But it could have been made by a bracelet being removed forcibly. Say, in a hurry, the bracelet was jerked up her arm—whether she was alive or dead—the catch giving way and scratching her."

"I'll go along," Meier agreed. "But what good are you doing Weaver?"

Thursday looked at him. "The police give Weaver a dozen different personal motives for killing his wife. Right now my prowler theory falls apart because there's no indication of anything stolen. But if I could only prove there *was* a theft . . . well, Weaver's not a thief."

"Maybe not, but you're an optimist. Pragmatically, the bracelet doesn't exist, my boy, hasn't for nine months."

"We know better—or guess better. It's been hidden for nine months and was swiped two nights ago. Weaver's neck might be saved by a fast recovery."

"Oh brother," said Meier.

"Don't you even trust yourself? You're the big watchdog of the stolen goods market. I'd guess the bracelet will be back in circulation in a matter of days, probably hours. The guys who have it now are so hard up they killed a Mexican tart last night just for the money in her purse. How much is the bracelet worth?"

"Now you're talking facts. Five grand, open market. That means about two thousand under the counter, most of that going to the fence. Leaving maybe eight hundred clams for whoever heisted it."

"Eight hundred would look like a million to the boys who have it now. They'll fence just as quick as they can. And right here in San Diego too—nobody with a guilty conscience is leaving town these days, not with that police blockade. Who's the most likely receiver?"

"Six of one, half dozen of another. Johnny Yakel's well-known, so is Pete Grimse, or Lipsky." Meier frowned. "They won't appreciate any cop angle, Max. They got their reputations to watch. For that matter, so have I."

"We'll leave the cops out of this. You're out too, except as middleman. Tell them I'll carry the ball, even tell them why. Your buddies wouldn't want to handle those emeralds any-way, not with murder connected. Have them tip me if they're approached. Nice stakes, you know. Maybe you recover the bracelet—and maybe I snag the killers."

"Gee, that was fun. Now what'll we play?" Meier drained his coffee, saw Thursday's haunted expression and threw his arms wide in mock endearment. "Okay, Max, *okay!* Blow your nose now, and I promise I'll spread the word around." Grinning broadly, "In trade for which, you pay for the coffee."

Thursday didn't wait for Clapp's return. Instead he drove to his office where he hadn't been for nearly forty-eight hours. Two days' mail was on the floor inside under the letter drop. He stood at his desk, sorting the trash from the correspondence. Ivah Hecht's retainer check, which was the only item in this morning's mail, he locked in a desk drawer. The rest was routine, bills and queries.

Except one item. It was sandwiched between Hecht's enve-lope and a local business furniture circular which had arrived yesterday, which meant it had been dropped through the slot sometime between Tuesday noon and Wednesday noon.

Dropped by someone not a postman. For it wasn't a letter, only slip of paper torn from a note pad. The message was printed hastily as if the writer had written it against the wall out-side.

Come see me at once! B. W.

Thursday stared at it, held it up to the window light, stud-ied the quick simple summons with mounting excitement. Because he could think of only one B. W. among his acquain-tances, and that was Bliss Weaver.

CHAPTER 19

He kept turning the paper over and over in his hands as he turned the idea over in his mind. And a reckless grin gradually parted his lips, a grin too vicious to contain any real humor. He folded the note carefully into his wallet. Then he locked his office and rode the elevator down.

He paused at the newsstand in the lobby to buy a pocketful of cigars and inquire softly of Fred if there had been any inquiries for him. Fred hadn't noticed anything. One worried glance at the black headlines all around and Thursday reassumed his poker face and ambled out into the midafternoon heat. He stood on the curb, jostled by shoppers as he lighted a cigar. Then he took the note from his wallet, pretended to read it again, and put it away. As he lingered on the curb, he made no attempt to see who was watching him.

He fluffed up the red petals of the dead camellia in his buttonhole and strolled slowly down the block to where he'd parked his car. He drove off across the city, choosing streets with the least traffic. The smell of the harbor grew stronger. And now his gaze wandered everywhere, most frequently to the rearview mirror with its portrait of the street behind. From among the tangle of automobiles and darting pedestrians and lumbering busses, a kaleidoscope of objects that moved and grew and faded, one car continued to reappear in his wake. A ten-year-old gray convertible, its black top up despite the weather.

Thursday commenced grinning again, the same grin, and quit watching the mirror except for occasional glances to make sure the convertible was remaining faithful to him. He had little fear of losing it and let it choose its own trailing distance. The black-and-gray car seemed to prefer a two-block gap. But Thursday chose the destination.

As he reached Harbor Drive's broad concrete encirclement of the glassy bay, he stepped harder on the gas, teasing the convertible after him. He cruised rapidly past the shimmering prairie of Lindbergh Field and the military training installations where new uniforms marched endlessly. Finally he turned for Point Loma, the high-humped peninsula that guarded the harbor mouth.

Up the Point's steep streets he rambled, passing expensive walled yards of latter-day haciendas and the proudly immaculate brotherhood of new housing projects. As he followed Catalina Boulevard out the crest of the hump, the residences gave out and furry sagebrush closed in. The convertible was staying back out of sight now because traffic was rare but Thursday knew they wouldn't lose each other. There were no more turn-offs.

He rolled through an open gateway that said: U. S. Military Reservation. Straight Ahead to Cabrillo National Monument. Open 9–5:30 Daily.

Sagebrush, clusters of barracks, an ominously neat cemetery, deserted citadels of earth that had once concealed great long-range guns, now outmoded—and Catalina Boulevard came to an abrupt end about three miles beyond the gate, terminating in a circular driving area like a skillet. Thursday braked by the tiny park in the center of the skillet. Amid the park's shrubs and sand plants stood an old whitewashed building of sandstone brick. From its pitched roof rose an octagonal glass tower, surrounded by a circular iron-fenced catwalk. To the dome of the tower it was three stories high. A century ago its light had guided ships into the harbor. Today it was a scrupulously maintained relic. Although built by the United States government (whose workmen had incorporated many bricks from a ruined Spanish fort and whose light-tenders had fondly married Mexican women) it was popularly known as the Old Spanish Lighthouse. Its half-acre of ground comprised Cabrillo National Monument, the smallest national park in the country.

The view was magnificent but too hot for tourists today. Thursday had counted on that. His was the only car in the parking area, as he hurried up the path into the light-

110

house. The persistent convertible had not yet shown up.

Inside the old building, its brick walls offered cool shelter. Thursday ignored the anterooms with their racks of postcards and showcases of souvenirs and local sea life. He trotted up the spiral stairway. There were two dim flights of metal steps encased in gray wooden bannisters. Then he climbed an iron ladder with canvas sides and he was standing on the concrete floor of the light tower. He crouched within it, not venturing out onto the surrounding catwalk, protected from outside surveillance by the tower's chest-high iron base.

It was hotter up here, as he waited near the top of the ladder. The sun seemed to beat on him through all eight walls of glass. Then he heard an automobile purr outside, come to a halt.

Thursday began to talk softly to himself, the first words that came to mind, a questionable city ordinance regarding lone women on the streets. From below he heard the scrape of a shoe. Feeling foolish, he raised his pitch slightly and pretended to answer himself. And went on listening intently.

The sounds below ascended, the faint ringing of metal as someone climbed nearer. Thursday's crouched muscles ached for action as the unknown cautiously took his time. His mouth dried out with anxiety as he mumbled on, an indistinct senseless dialogue with himself, baiting his follower to the top of the antique lighthouse.

Then, on the final ladder, the pursuer stumbled noisily, gasped in dismay and scrambled about trying to retreat earthward again. Thursday lunged forward, grabbed down through the hole in the floor. His fingers caught in hair and he hauled upward vigorously. The unknown let out a squawk of fright as his head and shoulders were drawn up into the sunlight.

"Sucker," said Thursday.

He had a handful of brown curly hair, a view of a familiar young face, its red mouth astonished beyond sensuality or smartness now. The pale face of Arnold Nory, cash register thief and former employee of Bliss Weaver.

CHAPTER 20

With a tremendous heave, Thursday lifted the young man all the way up into the tower. Arnold Nory, screeching with pain and indignity, lit on his feet. Thursday let go of the hair, shoved him away, but Nory came bouncing back, windmilling his fists.

"All right," said Thursday patronizingly. He caught a fist in his right hand and spun Nory around into a hammerlock. He frog-marched the ex-clerk across the tiny floor and leaned into him so that Nory's face was pressed against the glass pane overlooking the sparkling ocean. He jacked the doubled-up arm a little higher for emphasis and said, "Who you following, kiddo?"

"I wasn't following you!" Nory protested, writhing. "I got no job, nothing to do, thought I'd do a little sightseeing. *You're breaking my arm!*"

Three stories below a hedge-clipping caretaker glanced up curiously. Thursday said, "Why, I haven't even tried to break it yet." He released the arm, let Nory turn around. There was a saliva smear on the glass where his face had been squeezed. "Now quit lying. You picked me up when I left my office, tailed me all the way out here, too far for coincidence." Thursday gestured indignantly at the black-topped gray convertible parked below. "In that flashy heap! You think I'm blind, for crying out loud?"

"Ah, you're crazy," panted Nory, his brown eyes at their most candid. "Me follow you?"

"Because you thought I could lead you to Weaver." Thursday took the note out of his wallet. Nory tried to pretend he'd never seen it before. Thursday shoved the fake message into the young man's open mouth and said scornfully, "You're pretty much of a fumbler all around, sonny boy."

Nory spit the crumpled note onto the floor. "Yeah, is that

what you think? Well, I notice you took off in quite a hurry, soon as you got the message. Just because you had the luck to spot me—"

"Easy to spot a phony. Especially when I don't know where Weaver's hiding any more than you do."

"That's your story."

"Sure. What's yours? Why're you so interested in finding Weaver? You're no friend of his." Sneering, Nory began to frame an obscene answer and Thursday, smiling implacably, slapped it back into his mouth. The sharp whack rang around inside the iron-domed tower. "Now talk nicely."

Nory wilted, his face white except for the pink of Thursday's handprint. He stammered, "Don't get rough, don't hit me like that, I'm not a fighter—"

"What is it you're after? Revenge? The reward?"

"That's it, both I guess," agreed Nory eagerly. "Never could stand that stuffed shirt, and the chance of making something off of him . . . I'm broke, you know that. I need a little go-money, that's all I had in mind."

Thursday eyed him keenly. "How very interesting," he murmured and Nory squirmed under his long inspection. Thursday chose his next words carefully. "Correct me if I'm wrong. This means you don't know how valuable the compact is. The one with the dragon on it."

With big-eyed wonderment, Nory began, "Why, no, I never thought it was—" until he realized what he was admitting. Then he muttered sullenly, "I don't know what you're talking about. I misunderstood for a minute."

Thursday grinned and turned and started lowering himself down the ladder. Above him, Nory said, "I'm not going anywhere with you. You can't make me."

"I have your signed confession of grand larceny," Thursday said, halfway through the hole in the floor. "But I don't want to be mean about it because I think you'll want to come. You're pretty clever for a kid your age and there's no telling what we can get done together."

With that idea planted in Nory's head, Thursday dropped

out of his sight. He trudged down the dizzying staircase, smiling to himself. In a moment he heard the young man beginning to climb down after him. Nory was a cowardly fool but also a greedy one, and Thursday intended to keep him delicately balanced between fear and self-interest.

And so the ten-mile trip back into the city was much the same as the wild goose chase away from it, Thursday in the lead and Arnold Nory following behind. Just in case, however, Thursday kept a close watch on the convertible, ready to swing around if Nory had sense enough to make a break for it. It wasn't necessary and after they had filed their cars in a downtown parking lot, Nory demonstrated why it wasn't. "What were you saying about some big deal, Thursday?"

"I figure you as a kid who shoots high."

"Well, no use being a piker." Voice lowered, "Then you *do* have some angle on Weaver, don't you?"

Thursday winked cryptically and led the way into the austere office building across the street. As they rode up in the elevator he remained cold to Nory's whispered prodding, shaking his head to indicate not now. Along a discreet hallway of frosted glass doors was the one belonging to Ivah Hecht.

A middle-aged perfect secretary ushered them into Hecht's private retreat, the usual sober-hued den of leather furniture and glass-cased volumes, its walls livened by framed photographic views of a trim motor launch against a Yacht Club background. The launch's name was *Maybe*.

Hecht struggled out from behind his desk where he had been studying with dull eyes the evening headlines. STRANGLER HUNT WIDENS. His rosy cheeks seemed to have caved in slightly since yesterday, and the bare scalp amid his white fringe had a grayish cast. A faint odor of whisky spiced the air. He included Nory in his cordial greeting though he plainly had never seen the young man before.

Thursday suggested the secretary be given the rest of the day off.

Hecht looked surprised. "Well, it's practically quitting time, anyway." While he was out letting the woman go, Thursday arranged two client chairs in front of the desk, facing each other. Nory sat down in one, with a questioning glance, and Thursday nodded.

Hecht bustled back in. "Man, what's the conspiracy—"

"Lock the door," Thursday suggested. Hecht gaped at him, then at Nory, but obeyed and hurried around to sit in his swivel chair. Thursday seated himself and took his time about lighting a cigar, fully aware of the tension he was building in both men.

"What's going on?" Hecht pressed him. "What have you found out?"

"Well, first I wanted you to meet Mr. Arnold Nory, an interesting specimen of his kind." Thursday gazed tenderly at the young man. "He used to work in Weaver's downtown store, up to last Monday when we caught him with his fingers in the till."

Shocked, Nory jumped up. "You can't take advantage of me like this!"

"Shut up and sit down. This is just among us three. I was saying, Nory made a good salary, darn good for a kid his age. But he needed more—to keep up with a high-spending girl friend. Go-money, he called it a while back, because that used to be her favorite term for it. And this same girl friend owned a compact with a dragon on it." He paused, his eyes still fixed on Nory. "Need I say that her name was Joyce Shafto?"

Nory froze, then did his best to grin. "Well—what about it?"

"Not a bad parlay, tapping Weaver's cash register to spend on Weaver's wife. Okay, so that's why the world goes round. You had dinner with the Weavers a couple times before the separation. You're a handsome virile lad and Joyce couldn't resist your type, I suppose. It's easy to put it together, even easier to document." Without changing tone or moving his eyes, he asked, "Did you kill her, Arnold?"

Nory had been half-preening, rather proud of his prowess

as Thursday had described it. He collapsed with a frantic, "No, no, I only read about it in the papers! I didn't even see Joyce that day—after I was fired I went over to Romaine's bar, ask them—I was there the whole evening when—"

"Funny you didn't even call her and tell her your bad news."

"I tried! I called all evening but she wasn't home," Nory stammered in fright. "I mean, I guess she wasn't home because she didn't answer."

Thursday frowned but didn't pursue the point. He spoke to Hecht but he kept gazing implacably at the cringing Nory. "Well, Hecht, here's the secret lover angle you were so hot for. Same classic stuff, the dashing young man and the older woman—I guess your confidential information was okay at that."

Nory laughed nervously. "She wasn't *that* old, you know. She was hardly past thirty and I'm nearly—"

"Not too old to appreciate a handsome pup like you, huh? Just old enough to keep wanting the joys of youth." Thursday sighed, smiling. "How was it, Nory?"

And Nory, built up again, winked with adolescent lewdness.

"There's the love angle, Hecht," said Thursday, an edge to his voice. He swung toward the attorney for the first time. "Exactly what you said you wanted."

Hecht was sitting stiffly on his chair. His tight lips held back the sobs but nothing could stop the tears that rolled down his plump cheeks.

CHAPTER 21

Thursday got up and investigated a door at one side of the inner office. It opened into a conference room, cramped with chairs and a director's table. It boasted no other doors and its windows were seven stories above Broadway's teeming traffic. "Nory," said Thursday, and the young man hurried to his side like a pet. "Wait in here."

"What's the trouble with the old boy?" whispered Nory suspiciously. "I don't know that I like it."

"I don't know that you have to," Thursday murmured to slap down his cockiness. And to needle his cupidity, "We'll come out of this just dandy, wait and see." He closed the door in Nory's face leaving him a prisoner in the conference room, and went back to Hecht.

The attorney had his elbows on the desk, his head supported by his fists, his moist cheeks squeezed up so that his face had an Oriental look. "Let me get my bearings," he said huskily. "Please."

Thursday sat down and waited, embarrassed. Finally he said gently, "We've got to talk sometime, sir. It is your heart or your pride that got busted?"

Hecht shrugged and blinked and wiped a coat sleeve across his eyes. "Both, at my age. Well, I don't have to guess what your opinion is of me."

"Don't worry about opinions, particularly a hired man's. I reckon there's one or two others have fallen for beautiful tramps. Joyce must have had plenty on the ball."

"Oh, I knew she had her faults but I thought that I was the one with experience, the one to forgive—because I was the only one who'd ever really counted with her. At first I'll admit I was suspicious, in spite of wanting her so badly. What could she see in me? Then, what I suspected was only kindness, I became positive was—well, lovingness, even passion. And all that while she was stringing me along, using that ridiculous youngster for . . . " He stared at Thursday beseechingly. "Is it really true?"

Thursday nodded. "I'm sorry myself, uh, about having to play it this way. I had a hunch but I was afraid to put it to you direct. You see, if you'd fired me, I'd lose my contact with the Weaver case."

"It's all right, man." Hecht didn't understand and didn't care. He blew his nose resignedly. "At least this was quick and sharp and conclusive. That ridiculous young chap—to think . . . How did you happen to have a hunch?"

"Well, you were obviously holding back, afraid of some consequences. And the compact—a man who knows so much about a woman's compact certainly must know the woman pretty well."

"I didn't kill her, Thursday."

"I know that. Neither did Nory—unfortunately. A team of prowlers did the job; everything points that way." Thursday chuckled humorlessly. "Everything except the evidence. The trouble is that Joyce not only screwed up her life, she somehow managed to screw up her death also."

"Not just her own life," said Hecht dully, gazing at his pudgy hands. "I'm a bachelor, practically the old-fashioned professional kind. I never wanted it different until I found Joyce. I suppose I was overdue for a bad tumble, the one I should've had thirty years ago or more. I knew I was a fool. I told myself the absolute truth. That she was only a silly woman, that she was Bliss's wife. It still didn't do any good."

"Truth can seem pretty unimportant at times."

"But, don't you see, this was much worse than just some old goat having his last senile fling." He ground out his bitter self-hate slowly. "Bliss was my client. I was representing him in an action against Joyce—all the while I was making love to her! Do you know what my profession thinks of that sort of behavior?"

"I can guess."

"It means disbarment, Thursday. I've worked a long time to arrive at this point, hard years the early ones—and I toss it all out the window for a . . . " His tired eyes wandered gradually to the windows, the soaring empty heights. "Now, that would be quick and sharp and conclusive," he said with a sudden peace in his voice.

"What, die for Joyce?" said Thursday, grinning. "I bet she'd laugh herself right off the pitchfork at that one."

Hecht snapped around, insulted. As his flush faded away, he grumbled, "Well, you're right, man. I'd cut a fine figure sailing through the air, she'd be bound to laugh. Evidently she's laughed before, she and that youngster. I'll get used to the idea yet. I ought to stop feeling so sorry for myself, hardly a tragic figure at my height and weight. Yes, Bliss is the one to think of—how I can make amends to him. Been so worried about my own equivocal position." At the end of that disjointed speech, he even worked up a wry smile.

Thursday felt relieved. "What was Joyce's angle? Was she working you to get Weaver to drop his countersuit?"

"Nothing like that. She seldom mentioned the divorce troubles and that's one reason I thought she actually cared for me. But I guess it was my money." He said sheepishly, "I did furnish her quite a bit. She was always short, it seemed."

"You and Bliss and Nory, all kicking in to her—boy! She must have invented ways of spending money they haven't even heard of in Washington." Thursday shook his head wonderingly. "Okay, so you're out a chunk of dough and a chunk of ego. The rest of it is just between us."

"It won't stay so confidential, I'm afraid. It's bound to come out."

"People see you together?"

"No, I don't think so. Our times together, we were seldom in public, never here in San Diego. Most times she'd meet me aboard my launch at the Yacht Club and we'd have dinner together there. We were both cautious. But—there's the compact."

"Don't tell me you wrote letters to her."

"No." Hecht smiled weakly. "I'm afraid that letter business was an out-and-out lie. Joyce never kept her correspondence in her compact; I adapted that bit from another divorce action. But there is something fully as bad. An inscription I had put in when I gave it to her. To Joyce With Love—Ivah—and the date. It's engraved inside the powder cover, not easily seen—caution again. But it's there, enough to ruin me when it's found."

"It wasn't with her things in the apartment."

"I was afraid it wasn't. When I didn't hear." Hecht groaned. "What did she do with it?"

"Was it valuable? Worth being stolen, I mean."

"Oh, it was expensive, beautiful work on the inlay. But I doubt—"

"Could she have pawned it?"

Hecht shook his head vigorously. "She still had it the night she was killed. I saw it, man. This Nory youngster was telling the truth. Joyce wasn't home the early part of the evening. She was up the coast with me at Carlsbad, we had a quiet chicken dinner at the Twin Inns, and I brought her back to Marcliff about eleven or so."

"Now that's odd," said Thursday slowly. "According to the Folks—are you sure about those times?" Hecht nodded. Thursday rose and wandered up and down the office, scowling. "What was she wearing? The green one-strap gown?"

"Not with me. She had on a blue suit and a white frilly blouse. She was carrying the jacket because of the heat."

"So she came home wearing the suit and then changed into that sexy green thing for the rest of the evening. Does that make sense?"

"Well," said Hecht painfully, "knowing what I know now, perhaps Joyce was expecting a late visitor, another man. Perhaps even . . . " He looked sadly toward the closed door behind which Arnold Nory waited out of earshot, then he looked back at Thursday. His eyes widened. "Man, what's the matter?"

120

Thursday was standing in the middle of the office, pounding on his forehead with his fist. He stopped and grinned ferociously at the attorney. "Solid concrete," he said and swore. "Harder than that. Solid idiotic granite. But it finally sank through. You want your compact back?"

"Certainly, but—"

"Boy! This won't clear Weaver, of course. But it might pull the bloodhounds off his trail—if I can swing it." He strode toward the conference room. "You bet I'll swing it. What a jerk! Me."

Hecht hopped up, face aglow. "Do you mean that *he*—"

"No, Nory doesn't have it."

Hecht's glow subsided. "Oh. Then where are you going, man?"

"I haven't any idea." As Thursday twisted the door knob exultantly, he laughed at the attorney's dim expression. "But don't worry—the compact will be there when I get there."

CHAPTER 22

WEDNESDAY, OCTOBER 3, 6:00 P.M.

"I wish you wouldn't keep looking at me like that," Arnold Nory said. He squirmed nervously on his bar stool, nearly knocking over his fourth highball. His gestures were getting erratic.

"Just thinking."

"What about? How'm I supposed to know what you're thinking?"

"About the mess you're in," said Thursday, smiling.

"I'm not in any mess. Don't you worry about me. Leave me alone."

"No, you don't have to make a mess of it. But you will. You don't have what it takes for the size deal I got in mind. It ought to work out in a mess of dough. But I'm afraid . . ." He didn't say what he was afraid of and Nory squirmed again and ordered another drink loudly.

It had been like that ever since leaving Ivah Hecht's office. One minute Thursday would speak of the danger Nory was in; the next he would dwell on the money to be made from the danger, until the younger man wasn't sure whether Thursday was justice implacable or a venal profiteer. And always, whichever string he plucked, Thursday's underlying theme was Nory's muddling ineffectualness, his helplessness, his inability to handle his own affairs. It was delicate work. Despite his placid omniscient smile, despite the cocktail lounge's air-conditioning, Thursday was perspiring. Nory had to provide him with a destination before he got too drunk to reason. He had to take Thursday where the compact was.

Nory's weak face was ruddy in the reflected glow of the pink-and-silver wallpaper with its zodiac designs. He raised his chin, staring pridefully at the hero he saw in the mirror, perhaps dreaming liquorishly of the conquests he'd made in this and other bars. Thursday murmured in his ear, "I'm worried about you, Arnold, you and the money. I know how to help you. Why don't we go somewhere quiet and—"

Nory gulped down his drink, stumbled off his stool and walked with dignity out into the evening. Thursday drifted after him like a guilty conscience. This was their second bar. When Nory stopped under a corner street lamp to buy a late edition *Sentinel*, Thursday was at his shoulder. "A thousand-dollar reward. Maybe more if you knew how to milk it. You deserve it, the risks you've taken."

"If there's a payoff, I'll be right in there," muttered Nory, edging off along the sidewalk.

"The chance of a lifetime for both of us. That's why I wish you'd let me talk with you."

"Well, go ahead and talk!" Nory shouted. "Talk your head off."

"In the middle of Broadway?" Eyes, hurrying past, found time to be curious.

The eyes frightened Nory. He mumbled secretively, "Another bar, across the street there."

"Sure, and who might be listening?" said Thursday softly. He fretted to be in that unknown room where was the compact; he was tired of ordering drinks he didn't touch. "Don't you know of any private place where we could work this thing out with no interruptions?" He saw fear struggle with cupidity on Nory's face and he said, "Big money, Arnold."

"Don't know if I should," said Nory hesitantly, and Thursday held his breath. "There is this place I stay, sort of off the beaten track, but I don't think—"

Thursday began to breathe again. Somehow he hadn't expected the destination to be Nory's own quarters. "Fine. Lead the way." He was already walking Nory back toward the parking lot where they had left their cars. "I knew a bright kid like you would think of something." And before he left him to climb into his own car, he threw a parting shaft, "Only don't get to thinking you're too bright. There's plenty for all— my way."

He sighed and rubbed his strained eyes as he trailed Nory's convertible across the downtown business section and up the gradual slope toward Balboa Park. Yet, though he had slept only five hours in the last twenty-four, had not shaved today or eaten anything except a cup of coffee, Thursday had to admit he felt good, intensely alive. The expectation of success buoyed him up.

Nory got over onto First Avenue, topped the hill and crossed a bridge spanning one of the many dark canyons that laced the city. He ground his tires into the curb in the middle of a gloomy block, and the silver numbers painted on the curb read 3020. Thursday pulled in behind and joined Nory on the sidewalk.

"This look private enough for you?" Nory inquired belligerently. Then he snickered. "Nobody's ever interrupted *me* here."

Thursday glanced around. On one side, shielded by stray eucalyptus trees, was a ghostly white stucco building. Over its driveway was a sign proclaiming it to be SELF REALIZATION. CHURCH OF ALL RELIGIONS. FOUNDER P. YOGANANDA. On the other side loomed an old frame apartment building, once a modest mansion in the neighborhood's beginning.

But 3020, between the two buildings, appeared to be nothing but a weedy lot stretching down the canyon side into the eucalyptus grove. Yet there was a path worn through the sere yellow weeds, and when Thursday walked over to its starting point he could see the corner of a shingled roof, tucked away in a fold of ground.

"How'd you ever find this gem, Nory?"

"A friend passed it on to me when he got married." Again the boastful snicker. "He didn't dare use it any more. You bet I keep up the traditions, though." He led the way down the rustling path, around the eucalyptus trees, and they reached the tiny cottage, weathered redwood with a heavy rustic door. Nory used his key and went around turning on lights in the living room.

Thursday raised his eyebrows. It was an ideal bachelor home, living room, kitchen, one bedroom with its door closed. The furnishings were as ordinary as he expected, the only fragments of personality denoting an adolescent prurience. On the wall hung a blue-toned nude work of printing press art, and a chalky nude statuette stood on tiptoe on an end table, and one lamp had as its foundation a Balinese bust of brown wood. A copy of *This Is My Beloved* lay on the bolsters of the studio couch.

Nory trailed Thursday into the kitchen, saying, "I got a bottle here someplace." He watched Thursday apprehensively, dribbling straight shots into two glasses. Thursday plucked open the back door and tried to pierce the canyon blackness, then closed it again and gazed the same way at his host.

Nory held out the glass to him beseechingly. "Quite a place, huh?"

"You must be lonesome down here."

"Well, I'm no hermit." He took a hasty step forward. "Where you going?"

Thursday smiled. "Thought I'd admire the rest of it. Any objections?" He pushed by Nory and his two glasses of whisky.

Nory dogged him into the living room, breathing anxiously. "I better tell you. Better not go in the bedroom just yet." He winked at Thursday's amused face. "Sure, you understand. My new friend—she's still a little shy."

"I'm your new friend too," said Thursday, and moved Nory out of his way. He opened the bedroom door and groped for the light switch.

The bedroom had gauzy curtained french doors that led out onto a small bricked area. Through the glass he could see the shadowy brush of the canyon slope and beyond that the twinkling lights of the harbor and the airplane factory. Besides that view, there was the blonde woman in the double bed. Her burnished light-golden hair trailed all over one of the pillows, framing her slack pretty face, a bit dissatisfied even with sleep. She was sleeping nude between the tangle of a single sheet.

The sudden illumination woke her squintingly. She sat up, stretched and yawned. Then she became aware of Thursday. She didn't scream or flinch. She only peered at him and pulled the sheet up over the points of her breasts and asked in a rather high voice, "Did you ever hear of knocking?"

He said, "There's a time and place for everything." He saw the packed suitcases at the foot of the bed. He said to Nory, "Planning a little trip on the reward money?"

Nory nodded and craned around Thursday's shoulder to see the blonde. "Alice," he said, "this is Mr. Thursday. He's a new friend of mine. Alice, he's going to help us."

"I'll bet," she said, studying Thursday's solemn face. Then, "Well, give me one of those, Arnold," and she appropriated one of the straight shots Nory held. She drank it off, made a cute face and said warmly, "I'm really very glad you've come, Mr. Thursday. We could stand some good advice."

She jerked the sheet loose from the foot of the mattress and managed to draw it around her body like a sarong as she slid out of bed. It fitted her slender curves like a sunburn.

"My best advice is to be careful with that sheet," Thursday said.

Without making a move to adjust it, she smiled provocatively at him. "Worried?"

"Not I—but you should be." Then it was Thursday who was smiling. "How does it feel to be a dead woman, Joyce?"

CHAPTER 23

WEDNESDAY, OCTOBER 3, 7:00 P.M.

After a dreadful spinning silence, the woman looked past Thursday to Arnold Nory, goggling in the doorway, and she bared her teeth to say, "You miserable jerk, you!"

Nory made his feeble effort. "Alice—what's he talking—"

"Shut up, shut up! You're not fooling him any. You're the fool, bringing anybody here, bringing a *detective* here." On her long slim throat, tendons surfaced briefly. "Oh, what a jackass!"

"Well, what could I do?" Nory flared up sulkily. "He'd've thought it funny if I hadn't. Besides, you don't look like you with your hair that color."

"Oh, go fix yourself another drink and quit bothering me."

Nory wet his lips, the liquor fuzzing the many righteous

arguments he had in mind, and obeyed like a punished child. Alone with Thursday, Joyce Shafto eyed him shrewdly. She closed her bitter mouth with a perfectly blank smile; Thursday guessed the smile was her shield against confusion at times like these. He waited for her to decide how to act.

"Max," she decided softly, and he nearly let out a nasty laugh. To her shallow mind he was merely another male animal; he represented nothing more imponderable. Well, he could play games too, for his own stakes. Though insulted at being classified with every other glandular dunce she'd ever encountered, he smiled encouragingly and she followed that up with, "I'm in such a dismal fix, oh, you don't know how fantastic."

Her helpless feminine eyes worked him over. He said, "Don't say I didn't warn you about the sheet."

She hadn't forgotten it simply because it was dipping lower than the lightly tanned swimsuit-level on her bosom. Joyce blushed, covering the whiter softer flesh. "Now you're teasing me," she murmured, considering tears. "How did you guess that I wasn't dead? I didn't think anyone would be that smart."

"Too many things didn't jibe—there seemed to be two Joyce Shaftos. There was a Joyce who assiduously marked the race entries in the morning paper but left the evening paper untouched. There was a Joyce who came home at a late hour in a blue suit and yet got immediately murdered in a green evening gown. Well, I could have missed those two points forever. But the autopsy report shows that the dead Joyce ate tamales for dinner—and I happen to know the real Joyce ate chicken." Thursday shrugged. "See? Only one possible conclusion: it wasn't Joyce Shafto who got killed. Who was it?"

"Oh, I thought you knew that too," said Joyce. "My sister Polly."

Thursday chewed his lip. "Sure—of course. A redhead in your apartment in your clothes . . . It would have to be your sister to account for the family resemblance. And that's why

127

the police haven't heard anything from Akron about claiming the body."

"Oh," said Joyce in tremulous relief. "I'm so glad the police don't know. You won't tell them, will you? Not yet. Please, Max."

He looked her up and down, pretending inward doubts when he knew good and well he wasn't going to tell the police yet. Not until he'd gotten the whole story out of her. He had a use for that story and he didn't want any slip-ups when he put it to work. Soon—the sooner the better. If she would talk willingly, not make him break her down slowly and use up Bliss Weaver's precious time …

"*Please*, Max," she whispered intensely. "I need help, strong help." She hadn't made up her mind whether to use the tears yet. "I'll die unless I get help." She swayed nearer to him, as if blown by the winds of misfortune, and breathed deeply. Then she sent a savagely annoyed glance over his shoulder. "Well, what are you doing standing there?"

Nory wavered sullenly in the doorway. "Nothing."

"Then do it somewhere else. Max and I are trying to work things out."

"It's my house," Nory muttered, looking at the carpet.

"True," said Thursday. He casually lifted Joyce's hand, smiled at its daintiness resting in his grip, toyed with her fingers. He inquired, without raising his head, "I don't suppose you two murdered sister Polly, did you?" He got the expected gasps of denial. "But the second strangling—the Mexican girl?"

"Arnold and I were together here all that evening, weren't we, Arnold?" Joyce's fingers stirred innocently on Thursday's palm, her voice little-girlish with candor. "I'm not really guilty of anything, Max. Nothing except being afraid and sure, oh, surely it's no crime to be a helpless woman, is it?"

"No, I guess not." He felt her fingers climb onto his wrist as he met her eyes, bolder and surer now. "If you gave me your absolute confidence—"

"I will! I will!"

"*In* confidence."

Joyce took the broad hint. Her fingers trailed out of his grasp, promising the future, and she walked around Thursday to take Nory by the arm. She pulled him into the bedroom, cooing, "Arnold, doll—you look awful pooped. Why don't you lie on the bed for a while and take a little nap? Max and I have so much to talk over. That's a darling boy."

"I am not awful pooped," Nory protested thickly. "You think I'm drunk, huh? What's going on here anyway?"

Thursday wandered out into the living room, knowing how the wrangle would end. He flipped light switches, so that only the lamp with the Balinese bust was left burning, lighting the studio couch with a cozy phoniness. He brushed *This Is My Beloved* onto the floor, took off his coat and leaned back against the bolsters wearily. He reflected discouragedly on how dumb Joyce must think he was. Here he was, unshaven, unhandsome, unable even to hold onto his own woman, Merle, who through dint of long acquaintance had come to appreciate his few virtues—yet Joyce Shafto would have him believe he looked like The Man to her. He snorted. From within the bedroom he heard her voice rise high in anger. "You'll do it because I say you will!" Then she came out of the bedroom and closed the door.

She stood before him, putting her hands on his rough cheeks and looking down into his eyes. She implored him silently that way and all he felt was a curiosity as to what draping trick kept the sheet around her. She whispered, "I've been praying, Max. Praying that you are my way out. When I woke up and first saw you looking at me, I had the queerest sensation that . . ."

There was more of such drivel and to hurry it he put his hands lovingly on her hips, drawing her nearer. He had thought he was beyond sensation but at the touch of her thinly clad flesh he felt a faint revulsion as if she were indeed the dead woman. She slipped down onto his lap so quickly that she didn't notice his impulsive withdrawal. ". . . Arnold's not strong enough," she was saying, "and now I need someone's strength as never before."

She had wormed into a kissing position and that was what she wanted in order to seal the bargain she thought she'd made. She hid her face against his shoulder afterward. "I couldn't help myself. I can't help myself now."

Thursday sighed, but not with desire. "You'll have to tell me about it," he said. "I don't know how much time we have left. The police aren't easy to shake off once they get the idea."

Joyce raised her head. "Oh, poor Polly!" she said without much feeling. "Such a dismal thing to happen to her. The first time I'd seen her in almost two years. It was a surprise, her popping in on me Monday afternoon." While the Folks were down on the beach, Thursday thought; that's why they didn't know about the sister. "She'd been on a buying trip to L. A. and she just flew down here Monday with only an overnight bag, didn't even wire me she was coming."

Then Joyce must have gone out to dinner before the Folks's return; all that evening it had been the sister moving about over their heads. And when Nory had phoned to bemoan the loss of his job, he would have been answered only by the sister. "But you went right ahead with your dinner plans anyway."

"Oh, I hated to leave her alone the very first night. But I *had* to, Max. This friend I was having dinner with—"

"Ivah Hecht."

"That's right—dear Ivah. You see, I needed some go-money terribly desperately and Ivah has been such a lifesaver to me in the past." She paused thoughtfully, her fingers at play again on the nape of his neck. "I suppose that believing me dead has been awfully hard on Ivah, but I didn't know what . . . " Her eyes widened with true fear. "Max—*my life had been threatened!*"

"Now who'd want to kill a beautiful creature like you?"

"You're just saying that," said Joyce, shivering. "How can you say it, with this horrible bleached hair and with no makeup . . . " She wore makeup. He could see its gentle aid at the corners of her mouth and eyes, disguising her discontent with her thirty-some years. "Ah, Max—"

He had kissed her brutally because he'd suddenly realized that this animal heat in his arms was Bliss Weaver's wife, which made the vicious circle complete.

"Who threatened your life?"

"It was my bookie! I promised and promised but I couldn't pay. Then they threatened to kill me! That's why I had to go to dinner with Ivah. But even he couldn't lend me anything this time. He was kind of flat, too."

"Didn't you tell Ivah about Polly being here in town?"

"Well—no." She hesitated. "You must understand why. I was afraid Ivah wouldn't try as hard to help me if he knew Polly was here. And she'd already turned me down. She never could see the fun in gambling, not for sour apples. And when I told her about the threats, she just laughed!" And Joyce herself laughed brittlely. "I wonder what she thinks now?"

"What time did Ivah take you home?"

"Oh, I don't know. After eleven, I'm sure. I'm not very good at time. He didn't take me clear home, you know. I always had him drop me a block away."

"And Polly was already dead when—"

"I was scared stiff! Of course, I knew exactly what had happened. Polly had red hair like mine was, and she was only two years older. She looked enough like me to fool anybody who'd never seen me. And they sent a murderer who'd never seen me! They killed her instead of me—Max, I nearly passed out cold!"

"Poor kid," he muttered, and thought of Polly. Polly had been left alone to play the television and dine on canned tamales while awaiting her sister's return. Polly had looked over her sister's wardrobe and had come upon the emerald bracelet hidden at the back of some drawer. Polly had tried on the bracelet, posed in it; the next step was to try on the green evening gown that matched it. She had removed her underclothes to insure a perfect fit of the sleek tight dress. The climax of her dragging boredom—Polly had paraded before the bedroom mirror, a lonely siren in a green bracelet and a green gown, until the strangler's hand had rung the doorbell at eleven o'clock.

"I know what you're thinking," Joyce half-whimpered. "Why didn't I call the police? Max, I didn't think, I *couldn't* think, I was so unholy scared. I just ran. Then later, when I'd calmed down here at Arnold's, I realized how safe I would be if I never went back. I mean—I *was* dead. As far as my bookie and the murderer knew, Joyce Shafto was dead. If I went back and was alive again, I'd have the same thing to face all over. I couldn't stand it!" She earnestly pressed her face against his. "Max, was I so horrible?"

Thursday drew back and regarded her benevolently. "You were just scared, that's all. But what happened to Polly's identification?"

She stiffened slightly but could read nothing amiss in his friendly expression. "Well," she amended, "I *did* have the presence of mind to go into the bedroom and hunt up her purse and take it along with me. She hadn't brought any clothes worth mentioning. I thought if the person who killed her made a mistake, the police probably would too." She paused and added simply, "Polly's face looked quite unrecognizable, you know."

To cover his chill at her gruesome inanity, he clasped her tightly, mumbling, "There, don't think about it." She didn't; she kissed his ear.

"I don't want to," she whispered. "I want to forget. I want to stay alive, forever and ever." She pulled back to take his face between her hands. The sheet collapsed to her waist and she knew it. She said, her gaze searching his, "You know this, don't you—that you, only you, could make me aliver than ever? I knew it, first seeing you. Save my life and—oh, Max!"

He was supposed to be wild with passion. Her long lifting sigh was the signal for new caresses, further and further, but he couldn't stomach the idea. He despised her. Monday night he had done a deliberate wrong and he had suffered for it, even insisted that he suffer. Monday night she had done a deliberate wrong and she hadn't suffered at all. Nor had she any intention of suffering. He despised her because he was jealous of her utter triviality. Nothing could ever hurt Joyce Shafto. There was not enough to her.

"Yes," he said softly, hoping it sounded like desire. "I'll take care of you, yes. I've never met a woman quite like you, believe it or not." He gripped her naked shoulders tightly. "Right now, Joyce, if we only had the time . . . But we've got to get moving. Where's your clothes?"

"How wonderful right now would be," she breathed. "But I suppose it's true about the time. We'll have our time later." She was already vacating his lap. "My things are in the bathroom, dry by now, I think."

He got to his feet.

"I've only had the clothes I ran away in," she insisted on telling him. "I'll be so glad when I can buy some more. There were only checks in Polly's purse." She was lighting a cigarette from the box on the coffee table, her back toward him, the white sheet aslant her hips. She looked over her shoulder at him, smoke lazing from her nostrils, a backside parody of Venus de Milo. "I'll be completely in your hands, darling," she said and made a kiss.

Thursday opened the bedroom door. He said to her, for Arnold Nory's benefit, "And you'll get used to my hands, dear."

"I'll love them." She stood very still, smiling back at him.

Thursday went into the bedroom and closed the door. Nory was lying face down on the bed, his head cradled in his arms. His empty glass lay on the floor. He mumbled profanity without showing his face. "I heard you kissing her!"

With a pitying laugh, Thursday strode on into the bathroom, which smelled of recent nausea. Joyce's blue-tinted stockings and white nylon lingerie hung from the shower curtain rod. With one hand trailing the flimsy things, he wheeled back into the bedroom and proceeded to the bureau.

Nory still refused to look at him.

"Now I've got to get her dressed," said Thursday cheerfully. On top of the bureau lay two purses, Joyce's and Polly's. "She wanted her makeup too." He dumped out both purses quickly and in the second heap of feminine trinkets he saw the compact. Golden and octagonal, with a multi-colored dragon inlaid in an S-shape. He clicked it open, thumbnailed up the brass powder cover and read the inscription: To Joyce With Love—Ivah—and a date scarcely two weeks old. Thursday grinned in satisfaction, snapped the compact shut and dropped it in his trousers pocket.

He had made the recovery and fulfilled his duty to his client. He could do no more for Hecht. The attorney himself would have to work out the other aspects of his dilemma. Joyce might choose to drag Hecht's name through the mud with her—but the woman apparently had an affectionate, if dispassionate, regard for the old man.

Thursday said to Nory, "Look here, buster." Nory turned his head and one grieved eye peered up over his elbow. Thursday idly spun the gossamer white panties around in his hand, eyebrows raised smugly. "See how it is?"

Nory hid his face again, muttering indistinctly. From the living room, Joyce called, "Max?" Thursday laughed scornfully at the figure on the bed. Kicking the packed suitcases out of his way, he returned to the living room, closing the door behind him.

Joyce still stood with her back to him, cigarette smoke coiling in faint sensual streams around her nude body. "You took so long," she said with a gay nervous laugh.

"Testing my self-control. Not too good when you're nearby."

She gave him a sultry look as she bent to mash out her cigarette. She was good-looking, Thursday thought, watching her dress, but he had seen, and more frequently imagined, better. Merle was better, flatter of stomach, more graceful of thigh.

"I didn't find any slip," he murmured.

"I wasn't wearing any. Too hot. Nor any girdle either."

"Who said you needed a girdle? I didn't see your bracelet in your purse, either. Was Polly wearing it that night?"

After a false second, Joyce laughed shortly. "Oh, I don't have my emerald bracelet any more, Max. I used to but not any more. It was stolen, didn't you know?"

"I guess I didn't." Thursday wasn't surprised at her reaction. For her present predicament, Joyce could plead many excuses, fear, amnesia, kidnapping. But her concealment of the bracelet was plain fraud, an unmitigated crime. She wasn't going to admit that, not even to him.

"I suppose Bliss told you I used to have a bracelet," Joyce said. "Where is he, anyway? Why is he behaving so silly?"

"How should I know?"

"Why, I thought sure you knew where Bliss was hiding. The papers said you were on his side. That's why I sent Arnold to your office, thinking you might be tricked into showing where you'd hidden Bliss." A disgusted sound. "He botched it, of course. He was scared to death of you, after getting fired and all."

"Aren't you?"

"Not that way, darling."

"Arnold tried. The trick was no good because I'm looking for Weaver myself."

She sighed, sinking down onto the couch. "I've just got to get out of town, Max. I was afraid to try with all the roads blocked, police looking for my dear dratted husband. That's mostly why I wanted him caught, so *I* could get loose. That *man*—always spoiling things for me somehow . . . " She patted Thursday's head as he knelt before her. "Be awfully careful with those nylons, that's a darling. They snag so easily. And yes, that reward would have come in handy for me. I haven't any go-money *at all* and—is there any way we can use Polly's checkbook, Max? Oh, you pinched me, I'll bruise."

"Sorry. Maybe you better snap them yourself. Did you intend just leaving Bliss to be tried for your murder?"

"What a funny thing to say!" She snickered. "Oh, I wouldn't have been that mean. Though it would be a riotous joke on Bliss—and serve him right too, for that matter—but as soon as I'm absolutely safe I'll write the police or somebody."

Thursday doubted that she had any such intention.

She said, "Why, doll, your hands are shaking! Do I do that to you?"

He rose and looked down at her stockinged legs. She crossed them for him. He said slowly, "Well, you're not any cripple."

"What do you mean?"

"You're afraid of a cripple, aren't you? Buena Echavez. She's the one who threatened you about the money you owed."

"Buena? Oh, no—what's there to be afraid of in a *woman*?" She stroked the pale-blue nylon on her thighs, adjusting it to her liking. She straightened a leg, impressed by the curve of her calf. And yet, when she glanced up at Thursday an instant later, there was a flash of fear in her eyes. "No, it was a man who called me up about it, three times. The last time he threatened to kill me. He talked just like a gangster in the movies. But he was different—he was real!"

Thursday nodded at the confirmation. Buena had a backer, a man who occasionally visited his crippled investment via the backstairs. A bankroll who doubled in brass as Buena's strong-arm man. "Did he give you any idea who he was?"

"No, just a man, very brutal-sounding." Joyce, as she reflected, continued to make love to herself, pressing taut the material around her hips, cupping her breasts briefly as her hands rose to fluff her blonde hair. "Of course, it might have been that man, the one I saw come up from the beach several times. Out at Marcliff. I had the strangest feeling that he was watching me. But he was such a scrawny little fellow, Max—"

"With a bad scar on his mouth."

"That's right!" She stared widely up at him. "Have you seen him too?"

"I intend to." Abruptly reminded of urgency, he looked at his wristwatch. Nearly eight-thirty. "Where's your dress?"

"Help me up. In the closet."

Thursday opened the door into the bedroom. He was holding his breath; his scheme had taken perfect form so far. If only this one last detail . . . When he saw the french doors standing open, the empty darkness of the canyon beyond, he let out his breath through a grin of success. The packed suitcases at the foot of the bed were gone—and so was Arnold Nory.

He said to Joyce, "Come here a minute."

She peeked into the bedroom. "Why, the little stinker!"

"I guess he saw the handwriting on the wall. And we're too far below the street to hear his car."

Joyce said, "Oh." She rubbed gently against his side. "Max, I've thought of something," she whispered. "Maybe he's done us a favor. Maybe we can use this to help me."

"Maybe we can at that." Then he frowned. "Don't forget, Nory was your alibi for the murder of that Mexican girl."

She swayed to the closet, took a white ruffled blouse and blue skirt from hangers and began to put them on. "No, I was his," she said pointedly. "That's what I mean."

"Then I'll bet the police would like to hear about our friend Nory." Thursday smiled wickedly.

"Well, the police?" she asked doubtfully. Then her face cleared. "Oh, now I see. Oh, you wonderful guy! You have connections!"

He winked to confirm her assumption and went out to the telephone. Joyce followed, hopping along as she donned high

137

heels, and watched him dial. They grinned broadly at each other as he waited for the answer. It finally came.

Clapp sounded impatient and ferocious.

Thursday said, "Well, you've got time for this. I've got some dope on the strangler."

"Straight dope? Or is this another one of your half-cocked—"

"Get out here on the double. 3020 First. It's hard to spot but you'll see my car out front." Joyce was making frantic negative motions at him. "And bring your cuffs along."

"What are you talking about? You can't mean—"

"The heck I can't. I've got your strangler for you, boy." Thursday tensed his legs under him, ready to spring. "It's Joyce Shafto!"

CHAPTER 24

WEDNESDAY, OCTOBER 3, 8:30 P.M.

Joyce Shafto came at him like a cat, screeching in fury, fingers clawing. Thursday dropped the receiver toward its cradle and tossed the telephone directory in her face. That slowed her enough so that he could prison her flailing wrists in his hands.

A captive, Joyce screamed louder than ever and kicked his shins unmercifully. He pushed her backward, dancing to avoid her pointed toes, until she collided with the wall. The impact was enough to knock the bluish nude print off its hook, and its glass shattered on the floor.

"Quiet down!" Thursday ordered, and banged her shoulders against the wall a few times to show that he meant it. She did her best to bite him. Then with a deep breath, she unleashed almost every epithet he'd ever heard.

138

"That's better," said Thursday. "You're getting there."

Suddenly the rigidity left her body and she sagged helplessly. The only color in her face was that of her makeup. She made her last stand by trying to spit on him but most of it ran down her chin. She shrugged sullenly.

"Behave now," he warned as he released her wrists. "You want to look nice when the cops arrive."

She fell for the couch and lay there, glaring at him, mouth twitching. Thursday picked up *This Is My Beloved* from the carpet, tore out its flyleaf for scratch paper and began figuring with a stub of a pencil. He drifted into the easy chair across the room from her.

Joyce whispered. "And I let a filthy ape like you paw me."

"Yeah." In a moment, he looked up from his scribbling. "Well, you've got to take some punishment. Look what you did last Monday night."

"But I didn't kill Polly, you dumb goon!"

"No." His face hardened as he gazed at her. "But what if you've managed to kill your husband with your malicious mischief?"

"Oh, that's silly."

"Sure, a good laugh all around. Well, if I get your husband out of this, your Monday night stunt will cinch one thing. He won't have any trouble divorcing you. And he'll be able to do it cheap."

He went back to his figuring on the flyleaf. They made an unnaturally cozy scene in the dimlit room, he on the small of his back in the big chair, she stretched out on the couch, watching him. But her look was not of love.

Thursday was trying for his own information, to work out a timetable for the last hour of Monday at Marcliff, "Leaving the stairs clear for at least five minutes at a time," he muttered, "then . . ."

> Prowlers ring doorbell 11:00 (heard by Folks)
> Polly killed, bracelet
> taken

Prowlers beat it	11:05 (apt door left open)
Joyce visit	11:15–11:20 (approx Hecht evidence)
Weaver visit	11:25–11:35 (exact my evidence)
Thursday visit	11:40–11:50 (exact my evidence)
Mrs. Folk visit	12:00 (calls cops)

Looking that over, Thursday whistled despondently. He knew the timetable was largely correct but he had nothing tangible to back it up. It was far easier to believe the Folks's assumption, that Weaver had paid a half-hour visit, from the ringing of the doorbell to his observed departure. And only Thursday knew otherwise. He heard a siren in the distance.

"Joyce," he said softly. Her narrowed eyes hadn't left him.

"There's only one circumstance that may help you. Ivah Hecht, for some reason, loves you. He's a very loyal guy. So take my advice and keep your trap shut about dear Ivah and maybe he can guide you through this mess."

She didn't say a word. The siren wailed louder.

Thursday got up and put the timetable in his wallet. He went over to the front door and opened it as the wail died to a moan, then to silence on the street above. Feet crunched down through the weedy lot toward the cottage.

"What's this stuff about Joyce Shafto?" growled Clapp from the darkness.

"Take a look," said Thursday, and began turning up the living room lights. Clapp came through the door first, breathing heavily, and behind him the lamps reflected from the bruised forehead of Jim Crane.

Joyce sat up on the couch and tucked her blouse in behind, then smoothed the ruffles over her breasts. She gazed gravely at the open-mouthed policemen and then dropped her eyes demurely.

"Good—night—nurse!" grated Clapp. He spun around to his assistant. "Jim, tell me what you see!"

Crane was holding his head as if it had begun to ache again. "Well," he said feebly, "the hair's been changed but—"

"I'm throwing myself on you gentlemen's mercy," said Joyce, raising her moist eyes. "I can explain, I *want* to explain everything."

"Well, you certainly will be given every chance to try," snarled Clapp. "But right now I think I'll listen to Mr. Thursday."

Thursday recited an edited version of Joyce's assertions, omitting the bracelet and Ivah Hecht and Buena Echavez. Then he said to Clapp's bleak face. "The hard fact is that *the body was never really identified.* Everybody—including me; I'm not saying I told you so—went along on the easy assumption that the redheaded woman in Joyce's dress in Joyce's apartment was Joyce. There's a sisterly resemblance between the two women to begin with, and then you remember how the victim's face looked. Bloated, mottled, hardly human. You remember how little she looked like her picture."

"When do I have my head examined?" asked Clapp bitterly.

"True, nobody's going to win any medals on this one. But, Clapp, even her own husband didn't recognize that the dead woman wasn't Joyce. Weaver cinched the wrong identification when he denied that he had killed his *wife.* That wasn't doubletalk—Weaver actually believed Joyce was dead. So why should any of us strangers look for anything different? *Plus*— this little sweetheart made off with Polly's purse and identification." Thursday shook his head dolefully. "But if we'd been looking for the right thing, we'd probably have noticed a dress or coat in Joyce's closet with an Akron, Ohio, label in it."

Joyce had listened intently to Thursday's voice, her expression one of pleased relief since nothing he'd said had damned her so far. Clapp stood over her. "This all true, what he says about your sister's surprise visit?"

"Why yes, Officer, but he hasn't told you how I happened to—"

"Then take that blasted smirk off your face!" Clapp roared.

"When I think of the riding my department's going to get on this one, I could strangle you myself."

"Of course," said Thursday easily, edging into dangerous territory, "now that we know the real victim, it's not hard to pick the real killer. Joyce needed money for some bookie or the other; Polly had money. She wouldn't fork it over, they quarreled and Joyce killed her."

"Why, you ugly stinking—" yelled Joyce, springing up.

Clapp bellowed her down. "You speak when you're spoken to, or I'll put a gag on you! I'm in charge here and I'll tell you when you're in order." Then he grunted disgustedly at Thursday. "Max, you must think I'm pretty simple—and the way this case has gone, I can't say that I blame you. But you know no woman did the strangling. Those hands belonged to a man."

"You didn't let me finish," Thursday amended, feeling his way. All he wanted was to ease the pressure on the fugitive Weaver, make it possible for Weaver to show his face and be brought in safely. "Obviously, Joyce didn't do the actual strangling, as you say. I tab the boy friend—Nory—as the killer. Get the picture: a big argument at the apartment, Nory taking Joyce's part because he needed money too, a little physical persuasion on Polly that went too far."

Joyce gasped but Clapp's glance kept her seated and wordless.

"Nory's on the run but he can't have gotten far," urged Thursday. "Call off the hunt for Weaver and concentrate on Nory. Put out an all-points bulletin. It's my guess he'll blow skyhigh when you put it to him."

"And what about the Mexican girl? Did Nory kill this Zagal kid too?"

"He had plenty of girl friends," Thursday fabricated desperately. "I figure Zagal was one of them. She probably walked in here, recognized Joyce from the newspapers—and Nory had to kill her to shut her up."

Clapp looked across the room at Jim Crane. Then he hitched up his trousers cuffs above his ankles. "Getting kind of deep in here, don't you think, Jim?"

Crane smiled with one corner of his mouth. Thursday burst

out, "I tell you Weaver hasn't done anything except to be dumb enough to run away!" and at the same time Joyce squalled plaintively, "Doesn't anybody realize that *my life has been threatened!* That's the only reason—"

"Shut up!" When the room was quiet, Clapp growled at Joyce, "That's a good story too." To Crane, "If you think you can handle her, Jim, give angel face a ride to headquarters. Throw the book at her, everything you can think of—except murder. I'll go on with Max."

Crane walked over to Joyce and carefully handcuffed her right wrist. She rose, unable to believe the steel band she wore, quite unlike any jewelry she knew.

"But Nory—" Thursday began.

"Oh, yeah. Put out an APB on Nory, might as well get them all." Clapp smiled coldly. "But don't let it interfere with the search for Weaver. Come on, Max, you can drive me up to County Hospital, where I was heading originally."

"Not so fast," begged Thursday. "Let me tell you why I know—"

"No, let me tell you, son. The only trouble with your phony-baloney theories is that while you were fiddling around here with Joyce Shafto, another woman got strangled." Their eyes locked and then Clapp's dropped away. "This time it was Merle."

CHAPTER 25

WEDNESDAY, OCTOBER 3, 9:00 P.M.

Stein, the police medic, met them hurrying down the antiseptic corridor. The pitiless lights, his white surgeon's smock made his pointed ageless face swarthier than usual. His hands held two large gloomy X-ray transparencies.

"Well, thank heaven!" boomed Clapp, too loudly for a hospital. "Doc, will you get this madman off my neck and tell him she's okay? He won't believe me."

Stein quirked a sympathetic eyebrow. "Osborn's doing fine. The pictures don't show anything broken. I warn you, though, you can expect her voice to be husky all the rest of her life."

"She's doing fine," Thursday repeated to Clapp as if the other man were deaf. And he was aware of his whole body trembling, the idiot grin on his face. He felt dizzy enough to fall down—all because Merle was still alive!

Stein said, "Maybe I can give *you* something. You look worse than she does."

"No, I'm great, need a shave, that's all. Look, Stein, can I—can we see her?"

"I don't want her bothered, even while she's unconscious. When she does come to, I'm not going to let her talk, so forget it. Such bruises—like a gorilla had hold of her."

"Same as the others?" Clapp asked, and the doctor nodded. "Stein, I got to have a statement as soon as she's able to think straight."

Stein bristled. "Don't push me—or her, I'm the guy who says when." He tramped off down the hall.

Clapp took Thursday's arm. "Max, I'm due to take a look-see at the place she was found. If you want to stick around here, maybe find a cot to lie on or something, I can borrow your car . . ."

Thursday lifted his head. "You think I'm going to pass out on you? I just had a little reaction is all."

"Sure. I'm kind of fond of the girl myself. Let's go."

They trotted downstairs and across the hospital lobby. Spotting a phone booth, Thursday dived into it. "Out in a minute," he told Clapp. He dialed the Telephone Secretarial Service. He'd been out of touch for several hours and there was always the chance that Meier . . . but his phone answering service reported no calls.

Clapp was already hunched in the front seat of his car when he emerged. Clapp said, "No word from Weaver, huh?"

"Quit trying to outguess me." Thursday slid behind the wheel. "Where's this place we're headed?" Clapp told him and they roared off through the quiet old residences that respectfully surrounded the County Hospital. Thursday tacked on a southeasterly course to miss the downtown traffic signals. Both men were too full of thoughts to speak for a while.

Finally Clapp said, "What if it had turned out different back there, Max? What if Osborn had been as unlucky as the other two—would you still be so hot on saving Weaver's neck?"

"You keep forgetting. Weaver's not guilty. Joyce came home and found her sister dead even before Weaver arrived that night."

"Oh, cut it out. You know darn good and well there aren't any exact times to go on, especially that knothead Joyce's. Her homecoming time figures out as just before midnight, after both Weaver and you had left, and before Mrs. Folk found the body." He sighed. "A lot of traffic sneaking up and down the apartment stairs that last hour. But, I guess, anything can happen, will happen. Funny how life bunches up at the climaxes. Sort of in earthquake waves."

"Yeah, and add two prowlers at about eleven o'clock to start the earthquake."

"Oh, cut it out."

"Doesn't the fact that Joyce is alive cut any ice with you? What possible motive did Weaver have to murder Polly Shafto? You can't make the same case against him for that, as when you thought it was his wife."

Clapp spit pensively out the car window. "Close enough. Let's play Weaver went to Marcliff with the express idea of killing his wife. A redhead in that memorable green gown answers the door, he grabs her—the light was behind her—and before he sees who she really is, she's dead."

145

"You stick to that one, Clapp. Even Hecht can laugh that out of court."

"I hope it gets to court," Clapp said ominously. They were at the crest of Golden Hill and he glanced back at the lights of Broadway dropping behind them. "Mold it around a little. Weaver and Polly had an argument about Joyce. Again the green dress enters into it—bad associational memories and so on. Polly lit into him for the way he was treating Joyce. Weaver's thin-skinned and wouldn't take it."

"Why don't you just admit you're being bullheaded and be done with it?"

"Bullheaded? Well, maybe." They rolled down the eastern slope of the hill neighborhood into a glum district of small homes, aging too quickly. "Put your own prejudices aside a second, Max. Do you see what I've got to cope with? Three stranglings by the same hands. The first was Weaver's wife, or supposed to be. The third was Weaver's sweetheart. How can you expect me to say: well, Weaver, a jailbreaker with a record of violent outbursts, can't possibly be mixed up in this business. Turn at the next block."

Thursday pulled up at a faded rail fence that marked the end of a block-long street. He was parked beside a traffic patrol motorcycle, its radio crackling static, but there was no other evidence of police. From the dried-up lawns and from the lighted porches along the block, people talked and stared curiously at the street's end and the mysterious newcomers. They were nearly all Negroes.

Clapp and Thursday got out and leaned on the fence, getting their bearings. Below was a shallow murky canyon, uninhabited, but tonight pierced by numerous flickering beams—flashlights—and two steady spotlights from prowl cars. Through these shifting lights, men walked back and forth busily, and one instant's monstrous shadow gave Thursday a start until he made it out to be a horse.

Behind him the motorcycle's radio blared suddenly, "Repeat pickup order Number 31 . . ." Thursday saw the splintered board steps that granted pedestrian passage down and across the canyon to another dead-end street. Halfway down the near slope gleamed twin threads of steel, a single-track railroad spur, supported against the canyonside by a low wooden trestle that followed the land's natural curve out of sight. It belonged to the San Diego, Arizona & Eastern, a freight railway.

Thursday stiffened, alert to the radio. ". . . weight one hundred thirty pounds. Easy identify by large lateral knife scar extending from upper left lip to left cheekbone. Hold for question by Robbery Detail—"

"That's Scarmouth they're talking about!"

"Real name, Virge Paulus." Clapp smiled tightly at Thursday's amazement. "My doing, Max, but don't get excited. Leavenworth answered your telegram. Paulus was Gasman Lee's cellmate for a while before Lee died. He was paroled last month. Formerly a heist artist."

"But you been rattling on about Weaver and all the time you—"

"Slow down. Weaver's still the baby I'm after. I'm just doing what I have to do about Virge Paulus. I don't think he had anything to do with anything. But since a bozo of his general description was seen around Marcliff last week, what could I do? I turned it over to Robbery and they put out a want for him, just in case. If he's discovered to be in town, I'll talk to him too. Come on."

They picked their way down the treacherous wooden steps. Thursday was ready to burst with excitement. Virge Paulus, an actual name to say and conjure with; no more phantom theoretical Scarmouth, *Virge Paulus!* Virge Paulus and accomplice, you have been found guilty of murder in the first degree and this court holds no doubts as to the justice of that . . . Thursday, trailing Clapp down into darkness, chuckled savagely to himself. He would find Virge Paulus and accomplice. They were no longer figments of his conscience-stricken brain. His hypothetical killers were real now, the flesh-and-blood cornerstone of a theory he had scarcely believed himself. Despite Clapp's caution, Clapp's unshakeable arguments, Thursday knew at last that his theory was fact, beautiful, possible-to-be-proved fact. If Clapp would only concentrate the vast machinery of the manhunt on Paulus—but the official police thinking had been trapped and aborted by the dreadful insult of Bliss Weaver's escape.

Clapp turned left and Thursday followed along the canyonside trestle, stepping from tie to tie although the rail support had been filled in beneath with solid earth. A light suddenly shone upon them and a nervous voice cried, "Who's that? Halt!"

"Take that light out of my eyes!" snapped Clapp. The flashlight went off immediately. A man mumbled something in apology. As his eyes got used to the darkness again, Thursday could see that the flashlight owner was on horseback. "Who are you, what are you doing here?"

"Deputy Fairchild of Baker Company," the mounted man said. He carried a hunting rifle over his pommel. "Sunset Riders. You know, Lieutenant."

"Yeah, I should've guessed," muttered Clapp. "Where's Dow?"

"Gone somewhere, home, I think. Captain Gibson's in charge."

"Well, get that nag out of my way," rasped Clapp, and strode forward. Deputy Fairchild hastily spurred his horse up the slope to allow the two men to pass. Thursday could only catch tag ends of Clapp's growling phrases, ". . . if I had my way," and ". . . every last mother's son of them." Feeling keyed up anyway, Thursday laughed aloud.

A hundred yards from where the steps crossed the railroad tracks, a long-overgrown earthen platform had been bulldozed out of the canyonside. On it, close to the tracks, sat a wretched boxlike structure that had probably once served as a tool shed for line crews. Part of its flat roof had sunk in, only a few chips of its original stucco still hung on, and in the fierce glare of the spotlights, its naked weather-worn tarpaper and rusting chicken wire gave the impression of an exhumed corpse. It seemed the victim in the eerie scene, impaled on the beams from two patrol cars parked at awkward angles below on the little-used ruts of the canyon bottom. All around the bend and up the slopes wandered glimmering flashlights. Men called back and forth through the dark and sometimes a horse whinnied shudderingly.

Bryan came out of the doorless shed as they approached. His harassed look changed to relief as he sighted Clapp, but he shook his head to most of the questions.

"No sign of anybody, Lieutenant. All the men around here, there can't be even a rabbit hiding in this canyon now."

"I didn't exactly expect Weaver to wait for us. What you got there?"

"It was stuffed in under the mesquite, back of the shack there."

Clapp turned the red straw purse over in his hands. "Max, you know Osborn best. This look like anything of hers?"

"No. It's the Mexican girl's, isn't it?"

"That's what I figured, too." Clapp examined the pitiful contents, a dime-store lipstick, a handkerchief printed with a gay clown design, an empty satin coin purse with a bent catch. "No chance of prints on that surface. Try the lipstick container, though."

Bryan said, taking back the purse, "Did rescue a couple good footprints inside, a big man, left foot. They're making a moulage of them now."

"They ought to do to gas Weaver," a shadow grunted and clumped forward into the spotlight glare to become Chief of Detectives Pensic, while his shadow wavered up to play giant on the canyonside. His eye was better but his disposition wasn't. His coattail was slung back of the gun butt on his hip. "What about the Osborn woman? She die?"

Thursday drew Bryan aside. "Any chance there might have been *two* men hiding out in this dump?"

"Well—couldn't say, Thursday. We got footprints of one big man. The way the place got tracked up it's plain lucky we rescued anything."

Thursday nodded and hurried after Clapp who, with Pensic, had gone around the ancient shed to confront two men who waited there, part of the activity and yet, like the shed itself, not participating. Both were Negroes, the taller one middle-aged and conservatively dressed, with distinguished features. He was the darker of the pair and in the bad light his face was often nothing more than the reflections from his spectacles. The younger Negro's face had a yellowish cast, making it easy to read his fleeting expressions of fright. He wore a sweatshirt and faded khaki trousers on his stocky body.

"Lieutenant Clapp, police homicide," growled Pensic to them. "Tell him what you told me."

The older man stepped forward and took the floor with a resonant voice. "I am David Terhune, Lieutenant—Dr. Terhune. I'm the pastor of the Logan Heights United Christian Church. And this gentleman is Ebbie White, a member of our congregation." The young Negro nodded shyly and quickly returned his gaze to the silver coin he was flipping nervously between his hands. "Miss Osborn telephoned me early this morning—oh, I certainly hope that she's to be all right—"

"She will be," said Clapp gruffly. "But prayers won't hurt her any."

Terhune's thankfulness was visible behind his glasses. "All of us were very concerned. Miss Osborn has been our friend ever since she helped prove the innocence of young Hardaway—" Clapp nodded impatiently and Terhune cleared his throat. "This morning when she called, Miss Osborn wanted me to watch for anyone with a Mexican coin or coins. I was glad to help if I could, though I hardly expected—but at our six o'clock prayer meeting tonight a Mexican coin appeared in the collection plate. I notified Miss Osborn immediately and when she arrived we telephoned all of the members I could recall sitting on the lefthand side of the church. . . . Ebbie, you'd better tell the rest."

The yellow-skinned Ebbie shuffled his feet anxiously, almost a little dance. His reedy voice murmured, "It was just a mistake, me putting this old peso in the plate. I already traded the Reverend a real dollar for it."

"Son, could you speak a little louder?" requested Clapp. "Where'd you get the coin in the first place?"

"My store—Ebbie's Groceteria. Like I told the other gentlemen, first thing this morning I was sweeping out my store when this fellow come by. Big light-haired fellow, but I didn't pay much attention. He said he didn't have no change and he wanted to know if the peso'd buy him a pack of cigs." Ebbie White kept his gaze on the ground and only stole occasional glances at his intent listeners. "I told him I reckoned that was about right. So he took a pack of Camels and went off down the street. I thought naturally he was part of them street guys, ones been tearing up our pavement, but I seen him go down into the canyon instead." He dared a look at the policeman and was astonished to see that they believed him.

"Tell the Lieutenant about Miss Osborn now," Terhune prompted.

"After Reverend Terhune phoned me she'd be by, well, pretty soon she come and wants to know all about the peso. I told her same as I'm telling you gentlemen but she got all excited and strung-up. Didn't say much, just rushed off down the street, same direction the big fellow went." Ebbie glanced at the Mexican peso fidgeting between his hands and suddenly stuck it in his pocket. With a deep breath, "First off, I didn't pay much attention but then it suddenly come to me, started me worrying, a friend of Reverend Terhune's—a lady—poking around this dark old place at night. This was around eight o'clock and it just ain't safe, all the juvenile delinquents you read about in the papers."

Pensic laughed harshly. "So he followed down here, most logical route, and saw her feet sticking out of the shed. Weaver was already gone."

Ebbie blanched at the memory. "Yes, sir, that's how I saw her feet," he whispered.

After a moment Clapp came out of his frowning reverie and thanked Terhune and Ebbie White for their co-operation. When he excused them from further attendance at the scene of the strangling, they effaced themselves, Ebbie practically skipping away in relief.

"But we're getting close," rumbled Pensic, with a gesture at the canyonful of moving lights. "We'll pick up a trail yet, flush Weaver by morning."

He plunged away into the blackness again. Clapp and Thursday walked back along the tracks, shoulder to shoulder. "Hospital," Clapp informed him. As they started climbing the wooden steps, "You heard the verdict—a big lighthaired fellow. Just one."

"I still say there's two of them. It could have been Virge Paulus who decided to rob the Mexican girl or who decided to buy cigarettes with her money. Instead, it turns out to be Big Boy in both instances."

"And it just turns out to be Osborn who got herself strangled."

"No, Clapp. It could have been anybody who stumbled on their hideout. Merle wasn't attacked because she's Weaver's sweetheart—she was attacked because she was an investigator."

"Rubbish. Osborn tracked down Weaver and tried to talk him into giving himself up. So he throttled her. Soon as we get back to the hospital, I'll prove it to you."

CHAPTER 26

Back at County Hospital, Clapp grimly proceeded upstairs to argue with Stein. Thursday climbed into the lobby phone booth. His private dragnets had been out all day and he was certain there must be results because he wanted results so badly. And Telephone Secretarial Service reported two calls for him within the past half hour. The first was from Hal, one of his operatives—and the other was from John D. Meier. Thursday held his breath as he dialed Meier's home number.

"Oh, there you are!"

"What's up, John? Break it to me easy—you got a nibble?"

"Huh? Oh, you mean on the bracelet. No, nothing doing there. But on television, they had a news flash about your girl friend and I called to find out what was going on at your end."

"Oh," muttered Thursday. His face fell with his hopes. "Well, Merle's doing okay. I'm here at County, Clapp's gone upstairs to see if she can be brought to. No, I was hoping that . . . Call me direct if you hear anything, John, please."

His hopes fluttered up a little when he called Hal. But they sank to earth again. Hal had phoned to inform him that he was presently in bed with the measles and that he was sorry and disgusted that he wouldn't be able to work for a week or two.

Without spirit, Thursday trudged upstairs to find Clapp on one of the hospital phones. Both his voice and face were old and resigned. ". . . guess I understand how it is. Well, we're all doing our best. . . . Yes, sir, I'll call you first thing." He hung up.

Thursday slumped in an anteroom chair. The room was intended to be waited in. "What'd you get out of Stein?"

"A bawling out. But he's taking another look at her before

he kicks me out of the hospital entirely." Clapp picked up a magazine, slung it furiously into its rack. "I also got the word from Olympus. I called the Chief, hoping maybe he could do something about Dow and his vigilantes."

"Let me guess what he said. 'At this critical juncture . . .'"

"Yeah." Clapp picked up the magazine again, replaced its torn cover and put it neatly into place. "Well, mustn't be hard on the Chief. He's caught in the middle. How can he come out and say we don't want any action by private citizens—when three women have been strangled in spite of all our official precautions?"

"Somebody ought to do something about Dow. Somebody with a hammer."

"Tomorrow we'll be lucky if Dow's all we're saddled with. The Chief says there's been some wild talk about calling out the National Guard." Thursday let out a soft whistle. "Yeah, all for one lousy killer who's had the blind luck to dodge our net."

"Not one—two." Clapp made a disgusted sound and stalked to the far end of the waiting room. Thursday raised his voice. "Look, I've been right about a thing or two in this case, haven't I? Stop and think, what if I'm right about this too? Virge Paulus is the man you want—Virge Paulus and his accomplice, the big blond guy. Give it a chance, Clapp. Paulus took over Gasman Casey Lee's methods but he was too ugly to do the jobs alone so he added a helper, a man who women wouldn't instinctively distrust on sight." He held up his fingers, ticking off crimes. "Paulus cased the Marcliff job but Big Boy made the entrance and did the actual killing. I don't know whether Paulus planned the streetwalker robbery or not but if he did, he let Big Boy do the dirty work. That whole Ana Maria Zagal thing smacks of second-rate thinking; maybe it was strictly Big Boy's attempt to raise money. Merle—well, that wasn't planned at all, completely a spur-of-the-moment, self-defense thing."

Clapp was barely listening. Eyes closed, he murmured, "You know it all, don't you?"

154

"Everything except *where*. That's the problem. *Where* is Paulus & Company?"

Thursday came to his feet as Stein appeared in the doorway. Thursday asked, "There isn't any change, is there? She hasn't—

Stein talked to Clapp and Clapp alone, his dark eyes, glittering angrily. "I've got her conscious and lucid, Lieutenant, just what you wanted. If there wasn't a maniac running loose I wouldn't have considered it. I don't like to play around with patients as bad off as—"

"Don't take it so hard," soothed Clapp. "I left it up to you."

"Sure—the way you left it up to me, too." Stein slapped back his white sleeve to look at his wristwatch. "She's weak. I'll give you two minutes with her, not a split second more."

Then he briskly walked out on them. Thursday hurried after him. "She's really going to be all right, isn't she, Stein?"

Stein looked at him sideways. "I say yes. You want it in writing?" He stopped before a closed door and faced the two larger men. "Expect her to look sick. And don't jump out of your skin when you hear her voice. Don't let the poor kid know how bad she sounds. It'll sound like a voice again in a month maybe."

They crept into the sickroom, a small white cubicle usually used for detention cases. The window was barred, the furnishings spartan even for a hospital. The high iron bed nearly filled the tiny room and when the three men entered, the place was overcrowded. A green oxygen cylinder had been moved into a corner.

Merle Osborn was no more than a slim ridge under the blanket, a white face amid damply mussed hair on the pillow. She was too weak to have a personality, and she looked oddly small and defenseless in the formidable bed. When she opened her eyes slowly, even they seemed pallid, barely indicating that she knew she was not alone. A hot pang caught in Thursday's throat at the sight of her, at the sight of the bulky ice packs bandaged around her neck.

Stein turned on the lamp beside the bed and he touched her forehead with gentle fingers. Her eyes moved to the light for an instant then back to the doctor. "Merle," he said. "I brought up Lieutenant Clapp and Max, as I told you. Do you feel awake at all?"

Her bloodless lips moved but no sound came out. Stein wiped them with a damp cloth. Finally she managed, "Yes," in a whisper. For all its near inaudibility the whisper was a hoarse croaking squawk, as of two sawblades grating crosswise. Thursday shuddered; she didn't see him. "I'm wide awake," she said in that terrible new voice.

Stein stepped back and motioned the two men to the bedside. He glared at Clapp, holding up two fingers. Merle's eyes fastened on Thursday, pleadingly. There was little vitality in her gaze but the pupils were sane and clear, only bloodshot near the edges.

Clapp spoke softly and her eyes shifted to his face. "Merle dear, we won't bother you long. Just tell me this—did you see the man who choked you?"

Again the painful wrestling of her lips, again the rasping whisper. "Yes."

"Oh, fine," Clapp said like a prayer and he hunched nearer over her. "Who was it?"

In her gasping silence that followed, Thursday suffered with her. Then he became suddenly aware of her eyes closing, the tears squeezing out, and he felt as if he'd been hit in the stomach.

"I saw him inside there," Merle whispered in torture. Her voice scratched higher as if her nerves were ripping apart. "I saw Bliss choke me! *Bliss!*"

CHAPTER 27

Then she had fainted and the horror fled her face, and Stein was herding them out the door, swearing and saying, "She'll be okay, this was your idea, shove off and let me help the poor girl. Ssst—nurse!"

And Thursday stood dumbly in the corridor, staring at the closed door. He wiped his eyes and Clapp muttered, "Yeah, awful. Makes you want to tear something apart with your bare hands." An angry sigh and he started off. "Got to call the Chief. Promised."

"Wait!" Thursday grabbed him. "You're not going to tell him—*you didn't believe her, did you?*"

Clapp's mouth opened in sheer astonishment. "Believe her? Of course I believed her! She was lucid, Stein said so. You could tell by her eyes. She wasn't out of her head."

"You don't get the setup, Clapp," Thursday said desperately. "No, she was all right, talking to us. But she wasn't all right in the canyon when it happened!"

"Oh, for crying out loud—let loose of me."

"Listen, Clapp, just listen. For two days Merle has been under a terrible strain, the guy she loves accused of murder. She hasn't had any sleep to speak of. I've watched it happen. This morning she was beginning to believe that Weaver was a killer. Then it had to be her who tracked down the right peso, got that vague big blond guy description from the Negro. She went down the canyon tonight *expecting* to see Weaver. So when she ran into a man hiding in that railroad shack, she *did* see Weaver."

"You bet she did."

"Only in her mind, a delusion, a conditioned reflex. I tell you she didn't see anything, except maybe a big shape. It was black as pitch in that shack, you know that. She couldn't have—"

157

"Max," said Clapp softly, "take it easy. We don't know but what she was attacked out on the tracks and tossed into the shack. You're not making sense any more. Take it easy, try to lie down somewhere."

Thursday watched him walk away down the hall. I guess so, he thought dully. I can't be right when the whole world says I'm wrong. I'm sorry, Merle. I give up . . .

Behind him a woman's voice said, "Pardon, would your name happen to be Mr. Thursday?"

He turned quickly and an elderly woman in a gray-and-white supervisor's uniform had come up quietly on rubber soles. He said something incoherent.

"Would you care to use the phone in my office? The man wouldn't give his name but he said it was very important."

"Important?" He stared at her and a whole new life began. "Please—where's—"

"Right this way." She led him downstairs to an administration office with desks and filing cabinets. On the nearest desk a receiver waited off its cradle. Thursday snatched at it. "Hello, this is Thursday."

It was a man's voice, low and guarded. "Thursday the private cop?"

"Yes. Who's speaking?"

"You alone?"

Thursday glanced over his shoulder. The supervisor had vanished again. "All alone. Who is this?"

"A pal of John Meier's," the man said cautiously. "He told me to call you there. Maybe you know what about."

A throbbing in Thursday's ears, so loud he could barely hear his own voice say, "Was it—emeralds?"

"Whoo," said the man at the other end and gave a relaxing chuckle. "I guess I got the right guy."

"Spill it, spill it."

"This is Pete Grimse, I don't know whether Meier's ever mentioned my name or not. I got a joker coming in here

158

tonight to make a deal for a single rock. An emerald, sure."
Thursday started to cut in with questions but Grimse raised
his voice. "Look, this joker isn't anybody I know—he phoned
up cold—so I don't owe him a thing, get me? I don't want
trouble from any direction. Meier says this rock's got blood on
it and that's not for me."

"Don't worry, I'll handle it. When and where you meeting
this guy?"

"Here at my lot." He gave a downtown address. "In a half
hour sharp, eleven-thirty. You better get down here PDQ and
tell me how to play."

"I can tell you now. Soon as you hang up, step out for a cup
of coffee and stay out. I'm coming down now to step in and
take it from there."

"Mucho goodo," approved Grimse. "You're right, the joker
will probably case the place pretty careful before coming in.
He sounded nervous. Better hurry."

Thursday hung up and charged out into the lobby. He met
Clapp. "Business. Can you grab another ride home?"

"I'm sticking here for a while," said Clapp. He held Thursday back a minute. "If it's business about Weaver, son—steer
clear. I just got the word from the Chief. Weaver has been classified as a public menace. First sign of resistance or attempt to
flee, the orders are Do Not Allow."

"No. You can't. That's the same as saying—"

"Shoot to kill." Clapp's face was deadly serious. "Don't get
in the way, Max."

Thursday swore and ran down the hospital steps into the
sultry night. His car was parked nearly a half-block away,
near the ambulance entrance, at the end of a tall hedge of
eugenia that walled the dark grounds. The only other car in
sight was a gleaming station wagon. Thursday buttoned his
coat and sprinted along the driveway toward his automobile.
He had his hand on the door handle when a harsh voice
crackled, "Stop right where you are!"

Surprise, rather than the command, held Thursday motionless. The hedge rustled behind him. The voice said, "It will be easier if we go to where Weaver is—together."

Thursday turned around to face the hedge. The words, the overbearing voice, the station wagon, and particularly the ridiculous posturing, could only belong to Kelly Dow.

Dow's voice warned him tensely, "Don't try to pull a gun on me."

Ridiculous—but Thursday could hear the time ticking away on his wrist. He said calmly, "I never carry a gun. Don't you think you're being a little hammy?" He indicated the barrel of the shotgun poked through the foliage, pointing at his stomach. "Go back to your Wild West stories before you get in trouble. I got business elsewhere."

"Certainly you have," crowed Dow, and the shotgun didn't waver. "Bliss Weaver."

Thursday understood—and the sweat broke out on his forehead. Dow saw himself as a Man of Destiny. Only Dow was the man to handle things and he was taking his logical next step in the enforcement of his own brand of justice. He wasn't giving the police any credit for intelligence; he expected Weaver to make another attempt on Merle's life and he was guarding the hospital to bag the killer—and the credit.

"Take that silly gun off me!" Thursday snapped. "One of those twigs might pull the trigger."

"I think I can manage firearms," said Dow. "I saw the way you came running out to your car. You're staying covered until you take me to Weaver." He was no smarter than Joyce Shafto and Arnold Nory, who had believed the same thing.

Thursday's hands twitched in savage vexation. Time, precious time, sifting through his fingers and he stood helpless before this pompous egomaniac. Yet he was afraid of the shotgun because it might be caught in the hedge. "What've you got against Weaver, anyway? What do you think you're up to, Dow?"

"I hate cowards who murder helpless women," grated

Dow. "I hate those who help them get away with it. Don't move—I'm coming around now. And you're going to take me to Weaver."

Waves of cold swept through Thursday as the gun barrel withdrew, rustling, through the eugenia leaves. Then Dow's feet shuffled and his graying head looked around the end of the hedge, jaw truculent, the shotgun in sight again. He wore no white sun helmet tonight since it would have shown up too clearly in the darkness.

Dow stepped around the corner of the hedge, in full view of Thursday. The distant entrance lights of the hospital illuminated both men dimly. And Thursday stared.

Not at the shotgun or the menacing expression on Dow's face. But at the fringed leather jacket, at the flower jauntily thrust in its top buttonhole.

It was large and velvet-red and fresher than the identical blossom which hung wilted from Thursday's own lapel. A Princess Bacciochi camellia, Buena Echavez had called it. And Buena had called it something more . . . a Judas color, a Judas flower.

Tonight it was that, in Dow's buttonhole; a badge of betrayal on Dow's huge chest. In her own obscure fashion, Buena had labeled Kelly Dow with the mark she knew Max Thursday would read.

CHAPTER 28

WEDNESDAY, OCTOBER 3, 11:15 P.M.

Thursday laughed softly, and Kelly Dow skinned his teeth and thrust the shotgun forward. Thursday scoffed, "Put that thing away and stick to threats. They're more in your line."

"Just what do you think you mean?" Dow couldn't see the wilted flower Thursday wore because Thursday was only a silhouette to him against the scattered yellow hospital windows.

"I mean you're not the big secret you think you are. Clapp told me you were a dabbler and that fits you perfectly. Amateur soldier, amateur politician, amateur police force . . . and then you had to dabble at being a crook, too. An old gent like you acting like some thrill-crazy kid! For crying out loud, Dow, grow up!"

"You can't talk to me like that."

"I'm telling you facts and just like that," snapped Thursday. "You swell-headed nincompoop, you've been bankrolling a bookie joint for two years now. For two years you've gotten a kick out of playing crook, fooling everybody, thinking how clever you were at breaking the law."

Dow breathed, "I see I'll have to make things very tough for you, Thursday—"

"You're not going to make things tough for anybody, cowboy. The best you can do is pull out of San Diego and hope that the D. A. won't bother to yank you back. You can't threaten me the way you did Joyce Shafto." That brought a shocked grunt from Dow. "Sure, you were the voice on the telephone, talking like a movie gangster, telling her she'd be killed if she didn't pay her gambling debts. You scared her all right. But you never intended to follow through, it was all a big game to you. It wasn't so funny when you heard Joyce had actually been murdered."

Not so funny to his ex-carhop protégée, Buena Echavez, who had come to believe Dow had done it. She had decided to save her own neck by selling him out to Thursday; no doubt Buena was miles from San Diego by now. And Ivah Hecht, who handled some of Dow's affairs, had known about or strongly suspected his client. Yet Hecht had been afraid of Dow (or afraid of losing him as a client) and had tried to steer Thursday away from Joyce's bookie troubles. Surely Joyce had told Hecht of the threats—but the attorney had never mentioned them to Thursday.

And Tuesday night, the night of the Mexican girl's murder, Dow had paid Buena one of his nocturnal visits. Leaving, he had knocked out his pipe dottle on the back stairs, turned on the police radio in his station wagon—and arrived at Ranchers Market nearly as soon as Clapp.

". . . nothing to do with it!" Dow cried. "It was Weaver!"

"I've no doubt you honestly believe that. Just the same, you'd sleep easier if Weaver were dead, wouldn't you? That's why your morbid interest in this case, why you called out your riders, why you offered the reward. You want Weaver dead and the case closed. Because it wouldn't be so good if it somehow got out that the great citizen, Kelly Dow, had threatened the dead woman."

Dow eyed him narrowly, trying to remember what was done in situations like this. He edged the shotgun muzzle nearer his insolent prisoner's belly. "I wonder exactly how many people would believe this fantastic story of yours. If I thought—"

Thursday sneered at him openly. "Oh now, don't pretend like you're going to shoot. You're not the type and it wouldn't do you a bit of good. This is one time you're not on the inside of things, Dow. Your playmate Buena Echavez has been subpoenaed by the Grand Jury and she'll—"

"That's a dirty lie! *I'm* a member of the Grand Jury."

"Precisely what I mean," said Thursday coolly, playing the dirty lie for all it was worth. "A secret session tonight for the express purpose of—" He watched Dow's mouth sag open, his eyes widen as the incredible idea took hold. The shotgun barrel wavered.

Thursday leaped. His left hand slapped the gun aside and his right fist drove into Dow's face. Dow flailed over backward and his head struck the stone edging of the driveway. When the gun fell it blasted out a thundering shot, squirting up a cloud of dust from the driveway, and skidding buttwards several feet. Then both Dow and his shotgun lay absolutely still.

Such a racket was unprecedented in a hospital zone. It gave Thursday no time to hesitate. Already he could hear a commotion start in the hospital lobby, boil over onto the front steps. Thursday kicked the shotgun into the shrubbery. Then he hoisted the unconscious Dow like a sack of potatoes and hurled him into the back seat of his car. He couldn't afford to waste vital minutes in an argument he'd probably lose; nor could he leave Dow behind to continue to be a menace to Weaver.

As he sent his automobile spurting out of the hospital drive, Thursday thought he heard Clapp's commanding shout. He didn't look back to make certain. He chose the shortest route downtown and tromped on the accelerator. He didn't even think about speed limits.

The downtown streets were disturbingly deserted, only a few lonely sailors poking around. Thursday didn't see a woman anywhere. Because there was a strangler loose . . . The traffic signals blinked their colored lights for nothing; Thursday scarcely slowed for the red ones, hoping he wouldn't be spotted by any of the entire force of prowl cars he knew was on duty, trying to guard a half million people. The haunted feel of the empty avenues began to affect his nerves, the sense of panic and what-might-happen that was keeping people locked safe inside their homes.

He came to the address Pete Grimse had given him, a parking lot of gravel between two tall lightless buildings. Few cars were parked beneath its strings of naked bulbs, and the alley behind the lot was a mysterious tunnel of shadow. A windowed tin cube, set near the sidewalk, served as an office. It was lighted but empty; Grimse, following instructions, had vanished.

Thursday headed for the shadowy rear of the lot, parking his sedan quickly beside a battered relic of a touring car. A glance at his watch—it was already eleven-thirty! "Make him

164

late, make him late," he prayed silently. There was too much yet to be done. Only one emerald out of six had been mentioned, and it was unlikely that both thieves, Paulus and Big Boy, would show up.

Which meant he might need his car. Cursing and panting, he hauled Dow out of the back seat, opened the trunk of the adjoining touring car and shoved the big insensible body into it. From the size of the lump on Dow's head, Thursday didn't think he'd come out of it very soon. He hasped the trunk cover down securely.

Then, from the steering post of his own car, he snatched the registration slip bearing his name and hid it under the seat. He groped in his trousers pocket and did the same with Joyce Shafto's dragon compact.

And finally he was ready. He wanted to run for the little tin office but he made himself walk casually across the gravel, enter and sit down at the desk. He let out a deep breath. He slipped off his coat and draped it over the back of the chair. The little building was open to surveillance on all sides and he wondered if the men he sought were watching him from some nearby vantage point. Had he been delayed too long?

He leaned his elbows on the desk, listening, hearing nothing except the unusual silence of the city. He wondered if he looked enough like a fence to fool suspicious eyes. Rummaging through the desk, he found a green eyeshade and put it on in place of his hat. In the same drawer was a jeweler's eyepiece which he placed prominently before him.

The ledger on the desk top gave him an idea. He opened it and began to write hurriedly in pencil, hoping that what he was doing would look like business-as-usual to anyone watching. What he wrote was business—his own:

Grimse—call Meier—Meier call Clapp—K. Dow locked in trunk blue Stude—bankroll for bookie Buena Echavez—B. E. prob skipped town—K. D. threatened Joyce Shafto—J. S. may identify K. D. voice—Ivah Hecht suspects K. D. in bookie business, try for details—

He stiffened, pencil hesitating. From somewhere in the direction of the alley he heard a rasp of gravel, a cautious footstep, then another, coming nearer. Thursday scribbled hastily: *K. D. thinks secret session Grand Jury—scare him—*He halted and glanced up casually at the man in the doorway. "Just a minute, fellow," he said and made a final entry: *Virge Paulus arrived 11:40 p.m.*

He put the ledger to one side, still open, and covered the message with his hat. Then he leaned back in his chair and said, "Now, what can I do for you?"

CHAPTER 29

WEDNESDAY, OCTOBER 3, 11:40 P.M.

There was no mistaking Virge Paulus. The puckered scar on his cheek raised perpetually the left corner of his slightly sunken lips, revealing a tooth that was half white and half gray, probably a prison dental job. Small eyes glittered from under the brim of his hat, and the dark strings of hair that showed were threaded with silver.

Even in badly bagged clothes he was noticeably thin, as the witnesses had said. But by "little" those same witnesses had not exactly meant "short." Paulus gave an impression of littleness, just as his wedge of rough-skinned face recalled tales of witches, but he would have been nearly as tall as Thursday had his shoulders not been so badly stooped.

He had a cold. He wiped his nose as his eyes visited every corner of the small tin office and he said shrilly, "Who are you?" The unnatural level of his voice betrayed the rawness of his nerves. He was tensed to spring in any direction at a sound, at a touch.

"Pete Grimse," said Thursday reassuringly. "What's yours?"

"Okay, then." Paulus came a step inside the doorway, still taking spastic glances everywhere. "You don't sound quite like you did on the phone."

"We had a lousy connection. Where were you phoning from, anyway?"

"Never mind that!" snapped Paulus, staring only at him now.

"Well, don't explode," said Thursday easily. His own nervousness surged deep inside him in steady waves, not showing in his face or voice or hands, yet a fierce anxiety to seize Paulus, hold him, shout out for the police to come see. But there still remained Big Boy—Paulus must lead him to Big Boy . . . "Just making conversation. Want to talk about the ice instead? Or'd you rather go somewhere else to talk?"

"Yeah." Mention of the emerald seemed to stabilize Paulus. "I had to be sure you're Grimse." He came as far as the side of the desk; his bent shoulders gave his gait a crawling motion. "Yeah, let's talk about the ice," he said down to Thursday.

"I'll need to see it before I can make a price."

"I said I'd bring it, didn't I?" Paulus looked at the windows on all four sides of the office, then laid his fist on the desk top. His fingernails were dirty. His hand looked too lean and brittle to be that of the strangler. Crudely tantalizing, he kept his fingers closed for a minute, then opened them slowly and on his seamed palm shone the square green stone.

Thursday grunted unenthusiastically and Paulus countered with, "A beauty, isn't she?"

"Where'd you pick it up?"

"Used to be in a fellow's ring. Don't worry about heat, Grimse. You haven't seen anything about this one in the papers, have you now?"

"I'm not worrying." Thursday picked up the emerald, managing not to touch Paulus' flesh in the process. He screwed the jeweler's glass in his eye and tried in vain to focus on the gem.

Above him Virge Paulus was breathing erratically, saying, "I heard about you sometime back. Hesselman in Baltimore said you were a good egg. Now you don't see many rocks like that any more—worth a quick thousand if it's worth a cent."

Thursday removed the eyepiece and tossed the emerald on the desk top. Remembering Meier's evaluation of the bracelet, he said, "I'll give you fifty for it."

"Fifty, you said fifty?" shrilled Paulus. He wiped his nose and spit in the wastebasket. "You must be blind! Take another look, I never heard of such a rotten deal."

"Too much yellow tone in it," Thursday improvised in a weary voice. "It might make up into a nice marble for some kid but that's about all. Sixty's as high as I'll go."

"Sixty!"

"Sixty's the top. And that's only because you're a stranger in town and probably can't unload it anywhere else." He glanced up at Paulus through Grimse's visor. All in green, through the colored celluloid, the prowl thief's scarred face appeared ghastly and insectile.

Paulus snatched the emerald and told Thursday where he could go with his offer.

Thursday shrugged. "Suit yourself. It's a gamble on my side, buying it at all. I can't do much with one second-class emerald." He pretended to be struck with an idea. "Course, if I had three or four of them—a matching set—they could maybe make up into a good-priced piece of jewelry. But as it is . . ."

The bait dangled. Paulus seized it. "How much would you give me then? I mean, taking for granted I could lay hold of some more like it."

"Matching this one? That's hard to say."

"Well, you can make a guess. You know your racket, I know mine."

"Depends on too many things. If the match was good, if I liked the way they looked, why, I might be able to go a hundred, two hundred apiece." He watched Paulus finger his nose as he did the arithmetic. "That's a guess, not an offer. I'd have to see them first. And the certain market I got in mind is leaving town in the morning."

Paulus looked around desperately for a decision. "Well, I don't know, that's still not much payoff, considering. Well . . . maybe I should at least—" He stopped abruptly and made a gargling noise like a death rattle as he stared past Thursday toward the street.

Thursday jerked around quickly, ready for the worst. He saw what had stopped Paulus at the crucial moment. A black-and-white patrol car had nosed into the curb, both uniform cops jumping out of it. They closed in on a big man in a top-cat, passing on the sidewalk. Thursday couldn't hear the conversation but the big man dug in his hip pocket, produced a wallet which one cop examined while the other stood by warily, a hand on his pistol butt. The high tension endured for a full moment, then collapsed as the wallet was handed back. The topcoated man passed on. The cops climbed back into their car as if every bone ached, their gaze flicking idly over the parking lot and its tiny office.

"Looks like this strangler business has got the boys stirred up," Thursday said as he turned back to Paulus.

Paulus didn't answer. He was half-crouched on the other side of the desk, his insect eyes still fixed in dreadful fascination on the departing police car. Inside his coat, barely visible, he held a snub-nosed .32 revolver. It trembled.

Thursday eyed him narrowly, a bit grateful for the interruption. He hadn't known about the gun. A dryness in his throat told him how dangerous the scrawny bent-over Paulus could be. Fear, real or imaginary, might squeeze back that trigger at any provocation.

"As I said, this one likely market is leaving town." Thursday busied himself lighting a cigar to give Paulus time to put the revolver away. "Right now, it's the only bet I know of for emeralds."

When he looked up, the gun was out of sight and Paulus

was pulling himself together with an effort. But the blood hadn't yet returned to the flesh surrounding his ugly scar, and his perpetually lifted lip twitched convulsively. "Yeah," he muttered. "Yeah."

"If I could get a look at them tonight . . ."

"Well, if you got a car. No time like the present. You don't mind taking a little ride?"

"Not if I got to. Where we heading?"

Paulus' eyes glittered at the question. "I'll show you. Got enough on you to cover the buy? Not forgetting you may want to raise the price."

"I don't carry that kind of money, fellow. I can get it when it's time."

"How? Cash on the line, that's all I ever sell for."

"Don't worry, I don't use checks in my business. You show me what you got. If I like it, I'll call up and have the money brought out. That okay or not?"

"I guess." Paulus had put the emerald in his pocket. With a glance at the street, "Come on—let's get moving before . . ."

Thursday got to his feet, discarding the green eyeshade, collecting his coat, and shepherding Paulus out the door. Then he reached back and picked up his hat, leaving the ledger with its scribbled message plainly in view on top the desk. He strode quickly across the gravel to his car, Paulus close behind. Paulus went around to get in, passing by the trunk of the touring car where Kelly Dow was held captive. Thursday listened anxiously but no sound came from within the trunk.

Thursday stepped on the starter. Paulus said, "How come you don't lock up your joint?"

Thursday nodded toward the plate glass of a waffle shop across the street. A lone fat man sat at the counter with a soft drink. "I got an arrangement with a guy over there. Which way?"

"East. I'll tell you the turns. Guess you're used to night calls."

Thursday grunted, wheeling out of the lot. In his rearview mirror he saw the fat man emerge from the waffle shop, crossing the street. He prayed it would turn out to be Pete Grimse. He prayed that Grimse would see the ledger message right away, that he would act on it quickly when he did. With Virge Paulus riding beside him, Thursday overflowed with prayer.

CHAPTER 30

WEDNESDAY, OCTOBER 3, 12:00 MIDNIGHT

Before they got there, Thursday made a wild guess as to their destination. Virge Paulus had directed him along a circuitous route, turning and backtracking through silent city streets, while the scarred man kept an anxious watch behind them. But always their trend was eastward and when the last straggle of unlighted buildings had been replaced by brushy hills, and Thursday saw the fire glow against the midnight sky, he began to suspect the truth.

He was right. They left the paved highway and, at Paulus' instructions, bumped slowly over a rutted road into deepening gloom, nearer and nearer to the fires of the county dump. It was one of a half dozen scattered among the arid hills that ringed the city. Daily, trucks unloaded the refuse of civilization onto smoldering heaps and, nightly, the debris was prodded into new blazing life. Not as one huge pyre but as a series of volcanic cones since the dump was departmentalized, each species of refuse carefully piled upon its like. The dump covered two adjoining mesas, and it was into the slot between these mesas that Thursday was ordered to drive. The forgotten road was lighter now; above them the fires licked skyward from the cones; billows of red-lit smoke drifted slowly away, and the car jolted to a stop amid a picturesque castoff Hell.

"Right up here," said Paulus, and they scrambled out. They were at the base of one of the biggest cones where it had cascaded down the side of the mesa. Thursday's glance around revealed no sign of Big Boy or any other human being, and he had a sickening fear that his scheme had somehow miscarried.

But Paulus was commencing to climb, looking back for him, and Thursday hastened to join him. They trudged up the yielding slope, feet crunching deep into long-dead ashes and half-burned trash. This cone appeared to be the remnants of building materials as evidenced by blackened butts of lumber, shards of tile and weird globs of concrete. Thursday's ache of disappointment vanished as he saw their goal; a small campfire midway up the cone on an accidental ledge of rubble, its flickering light lost in the greater blaze above. A little lean-to of scorched tin signboards had been assembled there, enough shelter for one man—or possibly two—from the fine gray ash that sifted down like decayed snow.

All this Thursday saw in an instant and then his breathless attention was riveted on the man. He squatted by the tiny fire, where a blackened can of something was heating, his face musing over the primeval glow. His wrists rested on his knees, hands dangling. Huge reddish hands, their yellow-fuzzed backs wrought with bulging veins and tendons, fingers hanging down like fleshy lengths of pipe. Thursday nearly yelled at him with exultation. His arduous chase was over. Here squatted Big Boy, here at last was the strangler of Polly Shafto and Ana Maria Zagal and Merle Osborn.

At their approach, Big Boy sprang up agilely, backing away into the gloom, but Virge Paulus called out in a wheedling voice, "It's me, Olin! It's just old Virge, me!"

Olin crept forward again and looked across the campfire at his stoop-shouldered partner. His hand rose gradually, a big finger pointing at Thursday. He said, "Yeah, but who's he?" in a deep-throated voice of suspicion, tinged with a regional drawl.

In some ways he exceeded Thursday's expectations. He was more than blond; he was towheaded, the shaggy albinistic hair coursing back from his smooth sunburned forehead in two thick waves. He was not only handsomely innocent; he was baby-faced, rounded and soft of feature with sensitive lips and long pale lashes. And he was big, yet as wonderfully proportioned as a store dummy, heavily shouldered and chested, tapering healthily at the waist. What with the vertical chalk stripe in his stained blue coveralls, he seemed a giant. Huge as his hands were, they were only slightly out of proportion.

He was a perfect front man. Yet, on closer inspection, Thursday detected something wrong with his gentle blue eyes. Bland, unassuming—yes, but their small pupils seemed faded and devoid of life, empty of . . .

"It's all right, Olin," Paulus insisted heartily. "This is Mr. Grimse, the guy I phoned. You remember. He's all right, Olin, I'm not fooling you. He's going to take the rocks off our hands, give us money for them like I promised you." Behind his defensive reassurance sang a note that sounded to Thursday like pure terror.

"No, you never told me you was going to bring him out here," Olin said slowly, staring at both of them. He cracked his knuckles, stood there waiting for further explanation. Paulus swallowed audibly.

And suddenly Thursday understood the atmosphere of dread. The emptiness of the blue eyes . . . the unreasonable repetition of the brutal stranglings . . . The big blond man *was* a brute, animal strength uncurbed by human control. For Olin was little better than a moron.

Thursday's spine turned to ice.

"It just worked out that way, Olin, one of those things," Virge Paulus was saying, pleading almost. "He's an okay hombre, you'll see."

173

There followed a drawn-out silence before Olin grunted and Paulus relaxed. He muttered to Thursday, "Come on over and have a look." As Thursday followed around the campfire, Olin's empty gaze clung to his face, an appraising stare as impersonal as a hangman's.

Paulus was after something within the shelter of the leanto. The object clanked as he brought it forth, a mechanic's oblong tool kit of dented steel. It had evidently been stolen from a garage, for it bore smudges of automobile grease, the same that had left a mark on Joyce Shafto's rug. Paulus, kneeling, had opened the box. He beckoned Thursday forward to peer down into it. The wavering light caused random green gleams to sparkle within a compartment of the removable nuts-and-bolts tray.

Paulus was watching him expectantly, "Well, take a look, make me a price on them," he snapped. Thursday bent down and picked up the tray, causing the loose emeralds to rattle around. They had been broken out of their silver mounting. Thursday fingered them, pretending to scrutinize them while his mind worked fiercely. Here, on this desolate ledge, was everything he sought: the killers for Clapp, the emeralds for Meier, the balm for his own conscience. But now that he had caught the killers, how was he going to save himself?

Olin's voice, almost in his ear, made him jump. "Got a smoke?"

"Sorry," said Thursday. The supposed phone call for money . . . that would be his one and only opportunity. He would make his call to Clapp, of course—but what if Clapp couldn't be reached? Who else would understand his plea for help, necessarily cryptic, because Paulus would be listening to every word. He nodded gravely at Paulus. "They look better than I expected. I think we can do business."

Paulus sighed in satisfaction and looked up at his massive partner. "Hear that, Olin? He's going to give us good money for them. See what I told you?"

"I sure would like a smoke," Olin said meditatively but

there was a threatening rumble in his voice. He loomed over them like a storm cloud.

Paulus jumped to his feet and made a desperate pretense of searching his pockets. Then he looked nervously at Thursday. "Hey, Grimse, sure you haven't got a cigarette on you some place?"

"How about a cigar?"

"I don't like cigars," said Olin. "Why don't you have any cigarettes?"

Thursday remembered something, heeding the distraught expression on Paulus' face. "Seems to me there's an old half-pack in the glove compartment of my car. You're welcome to it if you want."

"Thanks," said Paulus. He turned to Olin and repeated what Thursday had said, as if Olin had not been present to hear it himself.

Olin said nothing. His eyes traveled from Paulus to Thursday to the gems in the tool kit tray. At last he grunted and turned and went off down the hill with long graceful strides. Paulus couldn't restrain a shudder.

"Nice playmate you got there," Thursday commented.

Paulus gave a quick look over his shoulder where Olin had gone. He wiped his nose and began to speak in a low tone, so rapidly it was hard to distinguish his words. "You must have connections, you're a right guy, I can see that. Do me a favor. I need help, nobody ever needed help like I do. You give me a hand and I'll pay you back somehow, maybe kick in my share of the take if that's what you want, only—"

"What's eating you?"

"I'm scared. I won't kid you—I'm scared." There was no mistaking his sincerity; Paulus was trembling visibly, apparently on the edge of breakdown, and the blood had drained away from around his scar again. "He's like that all the time, see? And all the time *he's getting worse!* I picked him up in Texas—needed a front for a routine of mine—and now I can't get rid of the big goof!"

"He's not so bright. Give him the slip."

"You don't think I haven't tried? But I'm strapped and he keeps the emeralds with him all the time, even uses the box as a pillow at night. I need cash but I don't dare take him out on any more jobs—he's ruined two of them now, an apartment job and we were going to knock over a cathouse, and he's just about to drive me nuts. He knows I want out and he won't let me! He says I'm the first friend he ever had." Paulus' shrill voice quavered and broke. "He—he'll kill me! Last night I woke up and he was petting my throat. He said he was wondering if I was thinking of running out on him—"

Thursday said, "I'll do what I can." It looked like a lever he could use.

Paulus grabbed his hand gratefully, skinny fingers slippery with perspiration. "I'll make it right with you, do anything you say. Only don't pull anything dumb. He's getting worse, I tell you, and there's no holding him when—"

"Shut up," warned Thursday. "He's coming back."

Olin reappeared on the edge of the littered bank. The thing in his hand didn't look quite like a pack of cigarettes.

"What you got, Olin?" Paulus inquired shakily.

"Look." Olin held the small brown shape up proudly. It was a wallet, fairly new. Thursday couldn't remember ever having seen it before. "I found it, Virge. It's got something in it, money, I reckon."

"Swell, swell," Paulus said, smiling and nodding at him. And to Thursday, "Now about the ice—"

Olin said, "I found it on the back seat of the car. I forgot to look for the cigarettes, though." He stepped nearer the campfire to examine the wallet. "See, Virge, there's money in it just like I told—"

He stopped suddenly and all three of them stared at what he held. The wallet had fallen open. Firelight glinted from the gold official badge pinned inside it.

Even as he stood numbed by the disaster Thursday understood the terrible trick of fate. The wallet belonged to Kelly

Dow, it had fallen out of Dow's pocket while he lay unconscious on the back seat of Thursday's car. The badge was Dow's honorary deputy sheriff's badge.

"Olin! He's a cop!" Paulus scrambled away from Thursday's side, pulling at his gun.

Thursday tried to kick the burning sticks of the campfire at the two of them but he was too slow. In one great bound, Olin was upon him, powerful fingers reaching for his throat, fastening there. Thursday went to his knees under the brute weight. Floundering awkwardly, groping blindly around in the ashy rubbish, he knew the meaning of utter helplessness. His entire body seemed to collapse inward, become strengthless, as the huge hands closed off his throat. He grabbed everywhere in panic as his eyes swam redly. His hand bumped a piece of lath and he flailed with it at the inexorable wrists, hammered with it, stabbed with it.

Olin's expressionless face was bent close over his, a mild gigantic face intent on killing him. Thursday heard the lath break, and the nightmare of his neck breaking with the same splintering sound. He jabbed weakly at Olin's throat with the ragged end of the wood. Olin winced, forward slightly and reached for the piece of lath, plucked it away.

Thursday, caught in only one of the deadly hands, sucked in a searing breath through his wide-open mouth. He kicked and writhed to escape. He caught a glimpse of Paulus, revolver pointed, circling for a chance to shoot. Then Olin captured his throat in both hands again and the terrible pressure didn't seem so bad now because reality was fading away.

The thundering blast awoke him. He fell to the ground, an excruciating torment in his right arm. But he could breathe again! Dazed and stupid with pain, he stared upward. Above, filling the sky, stood Olin. Olin was looking down, not at Thursday, but at his own hip where a dark splotch, slowly widening, had appeared on his coveralls. Puzzled, he turned his empty gaze across the campfire at Virge Paulus.

Thursday didn't know why. Then abruptly he did. Paulus

had shot him. The bullet had passed through his arm and had struck Olin. Not a serious wound, probably the spent slug had only lodged in Olin's skin, but . . . Thursday hoarsely shouted his last hope. In a rasping voice that seemed to be Merle's, he yelled up at the big man, "He's trying to kill you, Olin! He's trying to kill you!"

"That's a lie!" shrilled Paulus. "I was shooting at him, Olin! Listen to me! Olin, no, don't—*you big goof, it was an accident*—"

Scuttling backwards, Paulus dropped his gun. Olin caught him on the second stride and the scream of Virge Paulus died on a rising note as the hands found his windpipe. His feet, lifted clear of the ground, danced about and even kicked each other in frenzy.

Thursday crawled erect. His right arm went danglingly numb and he knew it was broken. He looked wildly for a weapon, saw the tool kit, seized its steel loop of handle in his left hand. He plunged toward Olin's back and began swinging the steel box at the pale-haired unprotected head. Once, twice, again and again—flailing blows that were mostly the weight of the tool kit, blows that seemed so pitifully feeble that the strangler wasn't even aware of them.

Without warning, Olin fell. He toppled forward like a tree and began rolling over and over down the ashy slope.

Thursday watched him go, staring dumbly till the rolling body came to a halt at the bottom and the fine gray dust settled gradually about it. Then he dared to drop the tool kit. There was blood on one corner of it.

The sight of Paulus, lying quietly with his head crooked at an unnatural angle, reminded Thursday of the revolver. He searched around for it. When he found it, he thought he saw a face high on the mesa above him, peering down, attracted by the noise. Thursday fired three careful shots into the air and the face withdrew hastily.

"Clapp," he croaked aloud through a throat that ached. "He'll get Clapp."

He sat down abruptly without intending to. He could see what remained of his strength running down his coat sleeve and he fumbled out his handkerchief to stop the blood. He chuckled dizzily as he pressed the square of cloth against a wound he couldn't feel. All was complete; it had begun with a handkerchief and now it was ending the same way. He thought of Bliss and Merle together. All because of a handkerchief. Merle, smiling from her hospital bed—and Bliss. . . .

Later, himself in a hospital bed, Thursday would find out about Bliss Weaver, about his time in hiding, the confused and desperate and soul-searching time. How he had hidden, from the first, without Hecht's knowledge, aboard the attorney's cabin cruiser at the Yacht Club. But now Thursday thought simply of the two of them united, Bliss and Merle. He scowled wistfully. That seemed to be what he had fought for; that seemed to be what he'd won, his Grand Prize. Why? he wondered. But then he remembered the grim alternative he had conquered.

"Clapp," he croaked again. "He'll have to tell me I made up for it, after all. I did, didn't I?"

He sat spraddle-legged in the ashes and debris, leaning the elbow of his broken arm on the tool kit, stubbornly keeping himself conscious. He heard the cry of a siren in the distance and he waited for the law to come and relieve him of his responsibility.